# SAVAGE

## A STEAMY, FORBIDDEN, POSSESSIVE, DARK MAFIA ROMANCE

### STRUCK IN LOVE ANTONIO AND SABRINA
### BOOK TWO

## CHIQUITA DENNIE

304 PUBLISHING COMPANY

Until Serena (HEA World Novel)
Antonio and Sabrina: Struck in Love 5
Heart of Stone, Book 4 (Jessica and Joseph)
She's All I Need
Red Light District (A Fantasy Romance Short)
Something Gaine( Romantic Comedy)
Upcoming Releases (2022/2023):
Aydin-TN Security Book 1
Dare To Love
The Carrington Cartel Book 1
Something Earned (A Romantic Comedy)
The Carrington Cartel Book 2

# DISCLAIMER

This work of fiction contains strong language and explicit sexual content and is only intended for mature readers. This story may contain unconventional situations, language, and sexual encounters that may offend some readers. If you're looking for sweet, fluffy romance, I would recommend another book. This book is for mature readers (18+).

# ACKNOWLEDGMENTS

I want to thank, first and foremost, God for giving me the strength to not give up and focus on not only my health and mental roadblocks, but also giving me the gift of storytelling. The most important woman in my life and biggest support system, my mom, Rhonda Dennie, my brother Brent Dennie, JD, Chris, and the entire family, without you and the family behind me none of this would be possible. Also, I would like to send a shout out to Elaine, Mercedes, and Kinney for helping me along the way in this author world.

# AUTHOR INSPIRATION

"*Never allow anyone to steal your joy. It doesn't matter how many times someone says you can't do something. Invest in yourself—even if it's just writing down what your goals and plans are. Starting small can lead to bigger things.*"

—Chiquita Dennie

# INTRODUCTION

I know your ready to delve deep into this book. I'm beyond excited for you to read and thankful that you've chosen my books as one of your favorites to include on your shelf. This book will cause you to scream, yell, laugh, and probably cry. Grab some wine and get ready for more spicy, sinful, sexy fun with.

Are you signed up for my newsletter?

Join today and find out all the latest in new releases, contests, giveaways, sneak peeks and more.

www.chiquitadennie.com

# SYNOPSIS:

Struck of Love never felt so good...

Sabrina Washington has worked hard to get what she wants in life. The last thing the sassy, headstrong VP executive wants is an alpha male who breaks all the rules, but when she meets Antonio De Luca, her steely façade crumbles under his gaze. He's exactly the kind of man who can unravel her straight-shooting reputation, and she's not so convinced that's a bad thing. As they grow closer, her ability to resist her desires wavers. Soon, she finds herself immersed in his sexy and dangerous world, and she's not sure she wants to go back to her old life.

# CHAPTER ONE

## ANTONIO

We arrived at one of our warehouses where we held meetings of a sensitive nature and kept supplies overnight until we could unload and sell to our offshore distributors. I was slowly controlling my temper before going inside and dealing with a major fuckup with a snitch who had been stealing from the cartel. More than a few heads would roll over this one. Opening the large stonewall door that was over hundred years old, I could still hear the rusty creaking noise. Bruno and I used to ask my father if this place were haunted. He just repeated, "Tony, the dead can't haunt what they can't see."

Many times, I'd tried to understand his meaning. It took me learning his world and role as the Don of the cartel to gain the perspective.

Nobody, there was no sound. Like a ghost haunting a house.

I reached into my pocket and checked my phone just in case Sabrina had texted me back from last night. I was wasting my time here when I could be laid up under her, wrapped in her arms and kissing her soft, sweet, chocolate skin.

Walking closer to the table, I began, "Gentlemen, we have a problem. It's come to my attention that we have someone telling our secrets."

Glancing around the room, I saw that everyone looked nervous. I quickly noticed Carlo coming in late as he nodded at me, and he noticed the anxiety in the room. Archie bit his lip. Danny was sweating profusely. Kane sat impatiently in his seat and checked his watch every five minutes.

"Are we keeping you from something, Kane?" I interrogated, staring him right in the eye.

I'd hoped he'd give me one good reason to end his life. I should do it just for fucking up my night with my baby.

"I'm not in a hurry, Antonio."

Kane looked me directly in the eye. I nodded back at him. I hope that let him know he was on my radar.

"We all know what happens to people that talk," My father smirked in my direction.

I glanced over at Bernardo Arturo as he started to speak. He was my father's second in command.

"Are you serious? Who's the piece of shit? Let me kill them with my bare hands," Bernardo spoke with so much anger.

"No need. We have our ear to the ground, and I've put someone in charge to take care of this situation before it gets out of hand." Father walked over to me and placed his hand on my shoulder. Everyone looked at each other and then at my father with a desperate look. "Bernardo, I've spoken with my son, and he will be taking on more responsibility, and it begins with this situation.

"Now, since that's settled, let's look at the numbers."

Before I could say anything, Bruno yelled out at our dad.

"He's too weak to handle something like this!"

"Watch your mouth, Figlio. Bernardo, you can begin with your area."

Before he could say anything else, Dad snapped his fingers for Bernardo to open the books.

"We have all of downtown coming in line with payments. My other concern is Derrick at the Lobby, and of course, the Italian deal," Bernardo dragged his hand across his face in frustration.

"Don't worry about that deal. It's being handled, personally, by Alfredo."

As Dad continued talking, Alfredo De Luca walked in, reminding me of the same attitude that Bruno has for me, and that he carried for Jimmy. He was Bruno's favorite uncle and Jimmy De Luca's younger brother. Alfredo walked toward each of us and kissed everyone on the cheek.

"Did I miss anything?"

Alfredo took a seat next to his brother. Dad nodded toward Bernardo to resume talking. I leaned back in my chair, closing my eyes to all surrounding noise. I was trying to block out the whispers and the yelling.

Carlo came and sat next to me.

"You're late," I hinted.

I wasn't too big on being ignored.

I noticed out of the corner of my eye, Carlo was fidgeting in his seat and looking down at his phone

"I need to speak with you," Carlo confided in my ear.

Suddenly not feeling like dealing with everyone, I rose out of my seat and started to speak.

"Bruno, at this moment in time, I couldn't care less what you think or feel about me. Our father put me in charge, and until he changes his mind, all questions, concerns, and deals will go through me, Capire?" When I was upset, I tended to lapse into my native tongue.

I narrowed my eyes at him and the surrounding men in this room. I never deviated my gaze. I was letting them all know that from this day forward, I was the new Don in charge. No one was to question me.

Suddenly, I heard hand clapping beside me.

Carlo stood up and yelled, "Il Nostro Nuovo Capo!"

"Our new chief!" he repeated, this time in English.

After that drawn-out meeting, shaking hands with the underbosses and my father, Carlo and I left the meeting and walked outside to our cars and got inside and headed to my family's home.

"Why were you late?" I requested.

"Camilla came to see me," Carlo explained.

I groaned in my seat.

This can't be happening right now.

"What does she want?" I inquired.

"It doesn't matter, Tony. I told her to stay away from you."

Carlo looked down at his phone again.

"Hot date or something? Who's texting you?"

"We need to keep an eye on your brother."

I nodded in agreement, not letting his abrupt change of subject divert me from his phone.

"Put Lenny and Sonny on it. Are you going to tell me who keeps blowing up your phone?"

Carlo passed his phone over to me, and I grabbed it. Looking down at it, I passed it back over to him.

"Tell her I'm not interested with the games. We're over," I ordered.

I leaned down in my seat, thinking about Sabrina and

how she would be mine real soon. Camilla better stay out of my way and not fuck up my plans.

Carlo nodded in agreement and turned his phone off as we headed over to my family's home for dinner.

I tried once a week to have lunch with Mom by herself, and she insisted we continue family dinner traditions. I could do without seeing my brother constantly berating my decision over not leading the family business. Also, keeping my foot on the legit businesses in New York. My father pushing me to get married into another Cartel family was about solidifying our legacy. The last thing on my mind was marriage unless it was with someone I chose.

Closing my eyes, I drifted off to my happy place of being with Sabrina.

"Bella, I miss kissing your lips," I declared.

"I miss you too baby."

"When are you coming home?" I inquired.

"I'm not sure, it's pretty busy at work today. We just closed a big deal." Sabrina countered.

"What are you wearing?"

"Antonio is that why you called me. Not to say hi, good afternoon, how's your day, like any normal boyfriend?" Sabrina joked.

"Babe, I haven't touched you in over eight hours, I need my fix."

"You are so spoiled," Sabrina responded.

"That goes both ways baby. Are you alone in your office?" I inquired.

"Yes."

"Touch yourself for me. I want to hear you scream my name." I urged.

"I'm at my place of business Tony. What if someone walks in or hears me?"

"Get up and lock the door."

*"You owe me for this mister. I want three orgasms and a foot massage later today." Sabrina said sassily.*

*I burst into laughter at the other end of the phone.*

*"Baby you can get as many orgasms as you want. I'd lick that pretty pussy all day and night. Just thinking about how sweet you taste. The thought is already making my dick hard."*

"Tony, did you hear me? Tony," Carlo jerked me out of my thoughts, nudging me in the arm.

"Sorry, what did you say?" I asked.

"Are you paying attention, or are you daydreaming about that Sabrina?"

Carlo walked up to our family home and opened the door. I walked in behind him.

"Focus on your own love life and let me worry about mine."

My mom walked in from the kitchen, and I greeted her with a kiss on her cheek.

"Ciao, Madre."

"Figlio mio."

After greeting me, she asked whether my father rode with us. As she was talking, I shook my head and took my jacket off and rolled up my sleeves. Grabbing my phone out of my pocket, I felt it vibrate. I was hoping that it was Sabrina. The only name I saw was Camilla, I rejected her call, and then I deleted her voice message. Blowing out a breath of frustration, I thought about my next move toward my Tesoro. That word had many meanings, and one of them was Italian for sweetheart. I was already calling her names in my native language. I was pretty sure that she would appreciate being called sweetheart in Italian.

Carlo kissed my mom's cheek and hugged her as my father and brother walked through the door.

"If I would have known you'd cheat on me with this little hoodlum, I'd sent him away years ago."

My father pulled my mom into a hug and kissed her soundly.

"Honey, you have nothing to worry about."

"I better not."

He smiled and gently kissed her forehead. He grabbed her hand and led her toward the living room.

Everyone followed and took a seat on the couch. My father pulled my mom onto his lap and rubbed her back while looking into her eyes and smiling.

The love they had makes me want the same things with Sabrina. I needed to work overtime on making her mine.

I was startled out of my thoughts by my brother.

"What's up with the meeting tonight?" Bruno asked.

I got up and walked over to the bar. I poured myself a glass of scotch, taking the time to try to get a hold of my next words carefully, so I didn't blow up on Bruno in front of Madre. Carlo grabbed a glass of scotch and began to talk to me.

"He was notified about a snitch in the Cartel. Starting tomorrow, we will put an extra detail on the family," Carlo stated.

"I asked Antonio since he's the new Don and all. Shouldn't he be suggesting all these new changes?" Bruno snapped.

My madre, shocked by Bruno's words, jumped out of my father's lap.

"What did you just say?" Mom questioned.

"Honey, calm down, you knew this was coming," Father said, trying to calm her down.

She slapped him across the face. Before she attempted to hit him again, he grabbed her hand. I tried to smooth over the situation by walking over to intervene.

"Mother, you have nothing to worry about. Father has trained me on everything, and I'm protected at all times."

I gave her a small grin, hoping that it helped put her mind at ease. She walked away from me and went toward their bedroom. My father sighed in content as he watched her. Knowing she was disappointed was the worst feeling in the world to him. Multiple nights, he talked about never letting a woman you love become disappointed in you because then you knew it would open her heart to someone else. "I have a lot of regrets in life. One is hurting your mother years ago. I refused her request," Dad said.

"What request?" I questioned.

"To stop loving her," he said and walked out of the room.

For the next half hour, we waited for my parents to stop yelling. Finally, they arrived with my dad hugging my mom around the waist and kissing her cheek.

"See why I should have been the new head of the family? You're always causing problems, little brother," Bruno instigated with a smirk across his face.

"Shut the fuck up, Bruno!" I yelped.

With my night ruined, I knew it was only a matter of time before my anger flared.

My mother walked over and kissed me on the forehead. I smiled back at her.

"Are you okay?" I pleaded.

"Yes, Tesoro. I'm trusting that your father has you protected with his life because he knows if he ever comes home without you, he has to answer to me. I don't play about my children," Mom stated plainly.

She sneered at my father. He attempted to make light of the situation by blowing her an air kiss. After waving him off and sitting down to eat, we all talked about our day.

Two hours later, we finished dinner with my family,

and Carlo followed me over to Ryde to finish up some work.

"Man, your mom scared the shit out of me."

"Everyone thinks my father is the intimidating De Luca, but get on Maria De Luca's bad side, and you've made an enemy for life."

We walked toward the bar, scoping out the ladies who came out tonight. I saw a few I'd take home to curb my appetite until I got Sabrina in my system. One of Nicki Minaj's songs, "Feeling Myself" played throughout the club just as I noticed a woman sitting by herself in the corner. She was drinking and nodding her head to the song.

As I walked over to her, Camilla jumped in front of me, effectively cutting me off from where I was headed.

"Tony, I've missed you." Camilla had to almost shout to be heard over the sound of the thumping bass line.

Camilla placed her arms around my neck and attempted to kiss me on the lips. I moved my head out of the way, and her kiss landed on my cheek. I wiped my face with a napkin, recoiling at her in disgust and moving out of her arms. Her eyes widened in disbelief at the show I was putting on in front of everyone inside the club.

"Don't think because we're currently broken up, you can just…"

I raised my hand to stop her from going further with her statement.

"Camilla, you cheated, and you've lied to me. I can promise you one thing, and this I take to my grave. Hell will have to freeze over and drag me back to the gates before I ever get back with you, let alone consider marriage," I informed her bluntly. Leaving her with her mouth agape in shock, I walked toward the lady sitting alone.

Five minutes later, I had Camilla bent over my desk, screaming and moaning my name.

"Shit… Tony… Ahh…" she barked out.

"Fuck… Sabrina…" I grunted out her name, forgetting it was Camilla that I was deep inside.

"Did you just call me by another woman's name?" She pushed away from me, and I fell back into the seat, making quick work of pulling up my pants and gathering my thoughts. I gathered my shirt off the floor and walked to the bathroom.

"Who's the bitch?" Camilla questioned, aggravation clear in her tone.

"Nobody." I slammed the door in her face.

# CHAPTER TWO

## SABRINA & ANTONIO

**S**abrina

It had been a week already since my last meeting with my father to discuss the latest accounts. He was late, but then he usually was, so I took a second to check my phone for the hundredth time that morning. Antonio still hadn't called. Yeah, I was crazy, and I should have just called him, but I knew he was trouble. My heart couldn't take another breakup. I should forget about Antonio De Luca. My gut told me to do just that. He was probably looking for a one-night stand, and I refused to fall into another trap. At the same time, I tried to follow in Janice's footsteps and just be more carefree. *Who am I fooling?* I thought to myself. I couldn't just have a taste of Antonio De Luca and not fall for his sexy, dominating ways. My heart was still fragile from Alex's cheating.

Finally, my father walked through the door. I stood and gave him a kiss and a hug.

"How are you doing?" Dad asked.

"I'm great. How are you and Mom?"

"She wants you to call her to confirm dinner on

Saturday with her and your sister Ashley," my father answered.

"I'll call later when I'm off. What's Ashley doing back in town?"

"Who knows? I thought you'd have a clue. I guess neither of us really pays attention to family dinners when in work mode." We laughed in agreement.

"Listen, Dad, I wanted to apologize for the other day in my office. I shouldn't have snapped at you. Alex was trying to get back with me by using you and Mom," I stated.

He waved me off.

"I'm sorry too. We shouldn't have gotten involved. You're a grown woman. You are perfectly capable of making your own decisions," he asserted, pinching my cheek and moving a strand of hair behind my ear.

I smiled at his endearing gesture.

"Thanks. So, let's get down to business, shall we?" I acknowledged.

"You want anything to eat? I can have Traci order in," Dad urged.

I nodded to go ahead and order as I gathered up my paperwork for our meeting, pushing the thoughts of Antonio out of my head for the next few hours.

* * *

ANTONIO

Entering the lobby of Washington Finance, I stopped at the receptionist desk. We'd come here once before and knew Spencer's office was up on the twentieth floor, but to avoid problems with security today, I followed protocol and let the receptionist do her job.

"I'm meeting with Spencer Jones. I'm Antonio De Luca," I stated, staring into the receptionist's eyes.

She stammered, "One moment… please."

After clearing her throat, she said on the phone, "I have Antonio De Luca for Mr. Jones." Turning to me, she instructed, "Yes, you're all set, Mr. De Luca. Head up to the twentieth floor, take the elevator, and go to the right." The receptionist pointed toward the doors of the elevator. We didn't speak as we rode it to the twentieth floor. A loud ping told us we'd reached our destination.

"So, I need to tell you something," Carlo mentioned.

"What is it?" I asked.

"When I was leaving the club the other day, heading to our meeting, I saw Bruno talking with Camilla. Then, last night, she popped back up at Ryde. I think they're up to something."

I could tell Carlo was getting angry. Whenever someone pissed him off, he'd grind his teeth. I needed to calm my irritation with the whole situation. I closed my eyes and pictured Sabrina under me, naked and moaning my name. If I found out Camilla and Bruno were working together in some way to hurt the cartel or me, my father would have one less body to worry about.

"Let's get through this meeting, and we'll handle Bruno later."

"You're already dealing with your dad and brother; we need the Spain deal to stick," Carlo stated.

"Yeah, we can't afford any distractions. I'll handle her. Let's get this going. I have plans later," I answered.

We entered Spencer's office. He shook our hands and motioned if we wanted a drink. Carlo and I waved off his offer and went to take a seat in front of his desk.

"So, gentlemen, I understand you own multiple clubs and other businesses, and you've just signed a deal with Spaniard Liqueur and Wine for ten million dollars?"

Spencer asked as he pulled up the information on his computer.

"Yes, that's correct. I wanted to get six million of that invested and have two percent distributed back into the clubs for more development and promotion."

Hopefully, he'd be able to work this through his company. The last thing I needed was the feds looking at my books.

"Sounds like a plan. Can I see the contract, so we can begin the process? Just so we have a clear understanding, the standard fee at Washington Finance is one point five million for all opening investments. Is that a problem?" Spencer questioned. Spencer narrowed his eyes at me, then Carlo, who had a smirk on his face. He thought we couldn't pull this off.

Carlo opened the bag that held two point one million in cash, and he handed it off to Spencer as I sat back with a wide grin.

"That won't be a problem, I can assure you," I said smugly.

Carlo poured everything out of the bag.

An hour after signing the paperwork, Carlo and I walked out of Spencer's office and headed toward the elevators. Suddenly, we bumped into a woman who looked all too familiar. Her papers landed on the ground, and we bent down to help her gather them. Snapping my fingers when it came to me, I recalled that she was Sabrina's friend Janice.

"I'm so sorry. I didn't see you coming," Janice muttered.

Janice grabbed the papers out of my hands.

"No problem," Carlo replied.

Carlo lingered onto the papers he was holding, trying to hold onto Janice's hand.

They both spoke at the same time.

"I know you," I mumbled.

"You've got to be shitting me!" she shouted.

"Excuse me?" I challenged.

**Sabrina**

Hearing a commotion outside our office door, my father stood and checked to see who or what the source of all the noise was.

"Who's making all that noise?" I inquired and started to get up to look for myself.

He motioned for me to sit back down.

"It's Janice and two guys standing by the elevator with Spencer. I think they're new clients."

Nodding in understanding, a small part of me hoped it was Antonio. I dismissed that thought since he didn't know where I worked or anything about me at all, for that matter. I sat back down and finished going over some new accounts with my dad.

**Antonio**

"Are you guys stalking me or something?" Janice placed her hands on her wide hips and snapped her finger in my face.

"I'm sorry about this, gentlemen. You must excuse Janice; she was just leaving," Spencer walked over and tugged Janice behind him, but she waved him off.

"Spencer, shut up, I know them. So, answer the question," Janice demanded.

"We have a meeting here. How long have you worked here?" I questioned.

Carlo walked closer toward her.

I looked around at the location and figured out the connection.

"Does Sabrina work here?" I asked.

I glanced around, looking at the doors, trying to

capture a glimpse of her. I noticed Spencer tensing up once I spoke Sabrina's name.

"How do you guys know Sabrina?" Spencer said suspiciously.

"Sabrina Washington is the heir and oldest daughter of Jonathan and Candice Washington. The Washington Finance group is her family's business," Janice informed me.

Carlo and I both looked at each other in astonishment. Spencer looked at me a little longer with an uneasy feeling.

"Listen, I wish I could stay, but I have another meeting I have to get to," Spencer stated as he quickly walked away from us.

Janice tapped Carlo on the shoulder, pulled him toward the elevator, and escorted us out of the building.

"This is such a small world. If I didn't know any better, I would say you planned all this," Janice suggested.

I could tell the flirtation between Janice and Carlo was just beginning as I continued looking around for Sabrina.

"She's not here," Janice told me.

"Where is she?" I requested.

"Antonio, we have another meeting we need to head out to before it gets late. Besides, you'll see her later tonight."

Carlo asked Janice for her number while I slipped into the car.

"We should do dinner sometime," Carlo proposed.

"Call me, oh wait… are you married, have kids, or a baby momma?" Janice rattled off a million questions.

Carlo leaned back and burst into laughter.

"Come to Ryde tonight. VIP on me, sweetheart. We'll talk over dinner," Carlo replied.

I noticed he winked at her, and she walked off, stomping her feet.

Carlo rolled the window back up, and the car pulled off. I pulled my phone out and lingered on our cartel PI's name, debating on getting info about Sabrina or just going back up to her office and demanding a conversation.

**Sabrina**

Ending my last meeting with a client, Janice walked in. She looked terrible.

"Ugh, bad day?" I asked.

She blew out a breath and flopped down on my couch.

"I met my future ex-husband," Janice said, bursting out in laughter.

"Girl, what are you talking about?" I questioned.

I got up from my chair and walked closer to her. I plopped down on the edge of the couch.

"You remember Carlo from the club, right?" Janice suggested.

Hearing a reference to that night brought up my earlier fear about Antonio. Feeling lightheaded, I walked over to the fridge and grabbed a bottled water.

"Your baby daddy was with him," Janice smirked.

"Girl, bye, I have no claims on anyone, let alone a baby daddy," I muttered

"Tell yourself anything you got to. If you must know, he asked about you," Janice replied.

"I didn't ask," I grumbled.

Rolling my eyes at her and sitting back down at my desk, I finished my daily work.

"Act crazy and nonchalant if you want to, that man is going to tame that little alpha personality you're holding onto," Janice boasted.

"First, no one is taming me. Second, I have no attitude, just no time for little boys. My motto is 'just sex' from now on. Besides, I learned that from you," I answered.

"Child, don't put your hoe ways on me. I rebuke the demon that opens those legs," Janice joked.

"Bitch, did you just say rebuke the demon that opened my legs?" I asked.

"Is water wet?" Janice opened her eyes and smirked at me.

I threw a pillow at her.

"I can't stand you," I told her.

"Tell that to my therapist," Janice said.

While shaking my head at her, she told me about her encounter with Carlo and Antonio.

"Are you going with me tonight?" Janice asked.

"I can't, Ashley's in town, so we're having a sisters bonding night," I answered.

Janice got up and picked up the pillow off the floor. After she was done, she placed her shoes back on her feet.

"Have fun for me tonight, and don't do anything I wouldn't do," I yelled out.

"In that case, I'd be a nun until the Pope decides birth control is like Advil for migraines," Janice joked.

We both convulsed in tears from laughing at her joke. Watching her walk out, I shook my head and got back to work. I saw Spencer knocking, wanting to enter my office. I yelled for him to come in.

"Come in, Spencer. Hey, what's up?" I questioned.

"Have dinner with me?" Spencer requested.

"Spencer, we've been through this, I'm not dating. I just broke up with Alex, remember?" I answered.

He leaned over my desk, making me increasingly uncomfortable. This wasn't the first time he had asked me out, and it wouldn't be the last.

"That's what I thought. So, no one has approached you about going out?" Spencer asked.

"What's going on, and why all the questions about my

love life?" I was getting pissed with this little random interrogation he was throwing.

"Nothing, I wanted to see if you've changed your mind as you promised me. You said when the time comes, you would call me first," Spencer argued.

His face softened in a vulnerable state. I felt bad for his one-sided crush.

"I didn't make that promise, Spencer. So, let's keep it strictly friends and co-workers; anything else would complicate things."

Spencer spoke again, but my phone rang.

"Hey, Ashley. Hold on one second." I turned to Spencer. "I'm sorry, I need to take this call. You need anything else?" I questioned Spencer.

"We'll talk later. Tell Ashley I said hello."

Spencer walked out and shut the door with a defeated attitude.

"Yeah, I'm here. She talked to Dad already. I'll be at the house on Saturday for lunch. Are we still meeting tonight at my place?" I asked.

"Yep, and I'm bringing the chocolate chip mint ice cream."

Finishing the call with my sister, I thought about what Spencer brought up and thinking about Janice's date tonight. I ended the last work call, closed out my email, and then left work to get ready for my date with my sister and a tub of ice cream.

# CHAPTER THREE

## SABRINA & ANTONIO

**S**abrina

I turned into traffic headed toward my place, thoughts rambled off about Antonio and if I should give him a chance or not. I lifted my phone and sent a text to my sister to cancel our get together. Finally arrived a few mintues later and parked in my spot, blew out a breath getting myself together, I headed up to my condo, and walked into my place. The smell of cookies hit my nostrils right at the door. I knew the only person it could be was my mom.

"Hi, Mom."

"Hi, darling."

"What are you doing?" I questioned.

"I wanted to see you. It's been so long, and you've been slammed at work. Thought I would come by and surprise you," she answered.

Placing my keys, purse, and coat on the counter, I walked over to give my mom a kiss and a hug. It took me back to when I was younger, and we'd sit up all night eating cookies and talking about my problems.

I finally released her and stole a cookie off the stove. "That's sweet, but I have plans tonight. I can't stay."

"Are Janice and Liz coming over? We can make it a girls' night," she suggested.

I headed to my bedroom to grab my robe. Then, I went back to the kitchen to talk before I had to get ready for my date. I plopped on top of the kitchen counter as my mom was cleaning up.

"I have dinner plans," I told her. This was the first date I'd had in over four years. I needed to calm my nerves down

"Really? That's nice, so do I know this person? It's Spencer, right?" she asked.

I rolled my eyes when she said his name.

"You're kidding, right?" I muttered.

"He's spoken to me about wanting to know what your interests and hobbies are. He likes you, what's the problem?" she asked.

"We work together, and secondly, I have no feelings at all for him."

I jumped off the counter and headed into the living room. I grabbed the remote to turn on some music.

"Fine, but he's not Alex, honey. You can't compare every guy to that bastard," she argued.

"Listen to you cursing." I laughed.

We both laughed as she gathered her things to leave.

"Listen, have fun tonight. No pressure, and I left cookies in the oven." I kissed her goodbye.

After she was gone, I went to the kitchen to turn off the oven and finish cleaning up. I heard my phone vibrating. It was a text message from Liz.

**Liz**: *Date tonight! Knock him dead.*

**Sabrina**: *Thanks, getting ready now. Let's plan on meeting tomorrow for lunch.*

I was dressed in a short, red dress with an off-the-shoulder strap. My hair was pulled up into a tight ponytail to showcase my neckline.

**Liz**: *I'll coordinate with Janice. Don't do anything Janice would do.*

**Sabrina**: *I promise.*

Shaking off any thoughts of sleeping with Antonio, I wouldn't expect much out of tonight, a free meal and drinks only. He seemed like the type to have a host of women in his phone to call for sex. A few mintues later I pulled up to the valet at eight pm to a restaurant named Antonio's. They took my keys and I stepped out and headed to the front door.

"Hi, I'm meeting Antonio De Luca," I informed the hostess. She smiled at me and escorted me to a private booth in the back.

**Antonio**

I was already sitting inside when she approached, and I gazed at her longingly, starting at her feet, moving up to the smooth shape of her curves and small waist, to her full-figured breasts, and ended up staring in her eyes. I had lost all thought and speech capabilities as Sabrina called my name.

"Antonio, is this one of the places you own?" Sabrina questioned.

"I'm sorry, what did you say?" I asked.

"I said, do you own this place?" Sabrina questioned with a slight grin on her face.

"I don't own it. My family does, and they named it after me. Please, have a seat." I gestured to the open seat across the table from me.

"It's a lovely place," Sabrina complimented.

"I think it's the second most beautiful thing I've ever seen." Sabrina blushed.

"What's the first thing?" she asked.

"You, of course."

"I think you've already had a few too many drinks. Maybe I need to catch up," she suggested.

"I can promise that I haven't had one drop of alcohol. Sabrina, let me be entirely honest with you. I usually just meet girls, fuck, and leave. However, there's something about you that's piquing my interest beyond my usual dealings."

"What am I supposed to say to that?"

I'd never felt this flustered before in my life, Sabrina thought.

"Say you'll see me again. What I'm feeling tells me you're different, and the feeling is mutual," I told her.

"Someone's very confident in themselves. We haven't even had the first date," Sabrina reminded me.

"I haven't been able to think of anything except you since we first met. I hope you feel the same way," I replied.

"I'd say that I just got out of something complicated. So, I can't say I'm looking for anything beyond tonight."

"I can see you'll be a challenge." I chuckled, staring into her eyes.

"Do you like challenges, Mr. De Luca?" she challenged.

"It's Antonio. I can tell you that I always get what I want."

"What is it you want?"

She leaned in closer over the table, making eye contact with me.

"You." Sabrina continued drinking her wine. "I know you want me as well."

"And how did you come to this conclusion?"

"You're sitting here with me, aren't you? Also by the shortness of your breath every time I touch you. The longing in your eyes for me to kiss you, and if I'm not mistaken, I can smell your arousal for me, even from this short distance."

Sabrina leaned across the table to whisper, "Maybe I'm just looking for a free meal." I laughed at her.

"At least it got you here."

I picked up the phone and called for the waiter to bring in the dinner. "I hope you like pasta; my family is famous for the pasta dishes."

"I love pasta, and it's a nice place. Does your family own a chain of restaurants?"

I gazed into her eyes.

"We have a few businesses, which brings me to you."

"What about me?"

"I didn't know Jonathan Washington was your father."

"How did you find that out?" Sabrina asked.

"I was at your company's office today and opened an account."

"Who did you open it with?"

"Spencer Jones," I told her.

Sabrina choked on her wine, visibly caught off guard by Spencer's name being mentioned. She immediately grabbed a few napkins off the table and wiped off her dress, my suit, and the table. I helped to clean up the mess.

"I'm so sorry. What time did you come in today?" Sabrina asked.

"Is something going on with you and this Spencer?" I asked.

"Why would you ask that?" Sabrina questioned.

"I just want to know if I have any competition that I need to dispose of," I said.

"That explains our conversation," she mumbled under her breath.

"What conversation?" I inquired.

"Nothing, just thinking out loud." Sabrina waved off my question.

"Sabrina, if something is distracting you, I need to know about it," I urged.

"Why?"

"Because I want your full attention on me. If anything, or anyone, attempts to get in my way of having you all to myself, tonight and beyond, then I want to take care of it right away."

"Antonio, let me be honest with you. I'm not the type of girl you would normally go out with. So, maybe we should just end this meal and go our separate ways before someone gets hurt."

I stared at Sabrina, brought her hand to my lips, and pressed a kiss to the back of it.

"I won't hurt you, but I can't stop how I feel. You can't tell me you don't feel this either. I'm a very controlling, dominant, and possessive man. If someone tries to hurt someone I care about, they will feel my wrath. I'm not saying this is a relationship yet. But I do want to explore this attraction we have though."

**Sabrina**

"Again, I say you may have made a bad choice on a date. I'm very controlling, a workaholic, and an independent woman. I'm not a size two like the women in your clubs, and if you haven't noticed, I'm black; not too many white guys are running around knocking on my door. I don't wait around for a man to figure out his shit. If you want to date me, then show me. Words alone don't charm me. I need action; trust is very important. Can you handle that?"

He looked at me with a smirk on his face and rubbed his hands together, seemingly eager to take up the gauntlet I'd just thrown down.

"Let's get out of here," he said excitedly.

"I drove here, remember, and did you not just hear what I said? Where are you thinking of going?" I inquired.

"Back to my place," he answered.

"I don't think that's a good idea," I said.

"Why? Are you afraid to be alone with me?" he stated.

"Has anyone ever told you that you have a big ego?"

"Has anyone ever told you that you're a smart ass, and I want to kiss you right now just to shut you up?"

I moved in closer to him and rubbed my hands up and down his shoulders.

"So, what's stopping you?"

Antonio ran his right palm down my right cheek. "I'm trying to be a gentleman about this, but you're making it very hard. Please… come back to my place. Nothing will happen unless you want it to."

"I think you'll be nothing but trouble for me, Antonio."

Antonio led me out of the restaurant and walked me over to a chauffeured limo.

"What about my car?"

"I'll have someone bring it to my place." Antonio answered.

"How about I just follow you in my car?"

"No."

"Why? It's easier that way," I questioned him.

"I don't want you having any second thoughts about coming with me. If you're alone with your thoughts, you'd probably just text me saying you'll take a rain check," he said, staring into my eyes.

Unbeknownst to him, my stomach was doing flip-flops from his stare down. I needed to take some control back.

"I think you're being a little dramatic."

Antonio told as he stood in front of me and stared into my eyes, as his phone continuously rang in his pocket.

"Aren't you going to get that?" I suggested.

I was agitated with this hold he had on me, and we hadn't even had sex yet.

"Damn," Antonio mumbled under his breath. "The only thing that's important right now is you, and they can leave a message if it's that important," he replied.

Antonio's phone continued to ring. Out the corner of my eye, Carlo ran outside just as he was getting into the driver's side.

"Hey, Jimmy is calling you," Carlo said.

"Shit, I need to take this. Sabrina, will you excuse me for one moment?"

Antonio took a walk to the other side of the restaurant to take the call. I could hear little bits and pieces of his conversation. Something about meeting up tonight.

*Maybe this is my chance to escape*, I thought to myself.

"Yes, I can't right now. I'm busy; let me send someone else," he said. Antonio walked back over to Carlo and whispered in his ear. He then pulled me into his big, strong arms and kissed me on my forehead. I couldn't help but blush at his protective nature.

"I have to handle some last-minute business," he said.

He looked disappointed that our date was ending early.

"I guess you're ditching me for a better offer." I smiled in a playful mood.

I tried my best to hide the disappointment that we were separating so early. Deciding to stick to my goal of no love, just sex, I got inside the chauffeured car as he talked to the driver.

"Make sure she gets home safe. If anything happens, no matter big or small, call me immediately," he ordered.

"I think I can get home on my own, Antonio. Thank you for a lovely evening," I spat out.

"Carlo, can you give us a minute?" he asked.

Carlo walked away and talked to the security at the

door. "When can I see you again? Let me make this up to you," he asked.

"I think we should just leave it as is; dating is a little complicated in both our worlds," I informed him, holding the strongest eye contact so he wouldn't catch on to the lies I was giving. Antonio held the door open, looking directly into my eyes.

"Don't do that with me," he argued.

"Excuse me? I'm not sure of the type of women you've dated, Antonio, but I can promise you I speak my mind. I'll see you around, Mr. De Luca," I snapped at him.

I slammed the door and rolled the window up. I didn't care to listen to any more of his excuses. He opened the door again and leaned directly at my face.

"I only have one type, and she's pissing me off right now. So, I'll call you tomorrow for dinner. Good night, Sabrina. The only time you'll call me Mr. De Luca is when I have you bent over on your knees with my dick in your sweet ass."

He pulled me gently by my chin and kissed me slowly on the lips, nipping at my bottom lip.

Opening my eyes, I thought to myself, he already left me horny, pissed, and wet.

"That damn man," I spoke aloud, rolling my eyes at no one in particular.

# CHAPTER FOUR

## ANTONIO

Morning came, and I sat in bed, thinking about the night we had that was interrupted by the cartel. Turning toward the clock on my nightstand, I decided to text Sabrina. Her little attitude had me turned on and pissed off all at the same time. If we had the chance to get back to my place, her ass would have been calling me Daddy.

I smirked and shook my head at the thought of her letting go of her control.

**Antonio:** Good morning, Beautiful.

Heading toward the bathroom and turning on the shower, I checked my cell for any replies.

*She's going to make me snatch her up*, I thought to myself.

Thirty minutes passed without a reply from Sabrina. I decided to try sending another text.

**Antonio:** I know last night didn't go as planned, but I want another chance to make it up to you.

I put my phone on silent and jumped in the shower. I let the water run down my back as I leaned forward. My mind filled with thoughts of Sabrina bent over, taking every stroke and screaming my name.

"Shit."

My dick was getting hard. I needed to think of something else before I caved in and called up a little relief. An hour later, I pulled up to the nightclub and saw Carlo sitting in his office.

"Did Camilla leave a number?" I asked.

"Antonio, leave her alone. It's not worth it," Carlo said. I motioned for him to keep talking as I attempted to keep all thoughts of the Camilla situation behind me and focus on business.

"So, we need to spread more promotions in the London location and build from that base. The turnaround may take about two years, but it'll pay off for our expansion plans. What do you think, Antonio? Antonio, are you listening to me?" he asked.

I was looking down at my phone when something was thrown at my face.

"What the fuck, man?" I yelled out.

"So, the great Antonio De Luca lives. Does this quiet storm have anything to do with Sabrina Washington?"

"I texted her this morning, but she hasn't responded. It's pissing me off."

"Wow, you have it bad."

"What the fuck do you know?" I snapped, ignoring his statement.

"Normally, it's just pussy. You don't get this worked up over it. She must really be special," Carlo joked.

"It's not like that," I replied.

"Then, how is it? I know a lot of guys who would love to trade places."

I glared at Carlo.

"Fuck this, I'm heading out. I need some air. I don't

need your opinion on my dating life. Just answer the question."

I knew he was looking out for me, but I was a big boy. Nothing would happen that I didn't want to happen.

"She said you had it already. How does Sabrina fit into the Camilla and the cartel plan?" he asked.

Waving his comment off, we changed the subject.

"How are the numbers looking from Washington Financial?"

Pulling the paperwork out, I started checking things out before deciding to move forward with a new club. The last thing I needed was my father trying to take control and selling one of my buildings.

"I guess the dinner is on hold," Carlo said.

"Not if I can help it if you must know. Can we get back to work? I want to have a meeting with Danny about expanding and looking at places in Los Angeles and out of the country, like London first."

"Okay, and what about the situation with the snitch?" Carlo asked.

"Bruno is handling it. He's hell-bent on some power trip of showing my father he should have made him the next Don of the family. Anyway, why are you so stressed about it?"

"I have my resources, Tony, and I'm your brother. I'm here to help in any way I can. Besides, if you get killed over this, your mom will kick my ass," Carlo told me.

"What's happening with your date tonight? It's with Janice, right?" I asked.

"Nice change of subject, but we made plans for dinner at Little Italy and then a movie, probably."

I noticed Carlo shrugged his shoulders.

My phone vibrated in my pocket. Taking it out, I

noticed it was Camilla calling. Since I had a few minutes before my next meeting, I could handle her quickly.

"Who's that?" Carlo asked.

"Camilla."

Carlo looked at me, disappointed.

I shook my head for him to be quiet, and I answered the phone on speaker.

"Hello?" I answered.

"Tony, baby, I need to talk to you," Camilla said.

"What do you want, Camilla?"

Carlo was getting out of his seat and walking toward the door. I snapped my finger to get his attention, but he left the room, completely ignoring me.

"Please, Tony, it's important," she begged.

"Are you crying?"

I could hear sniffling in the background.

"I need you, baby," Camilla whispered.

I closed my eyes and thought long and hard about the next words out of my mouth. Camilla was at one time, the love of my life. She was the woman I was going to marry. She couldn't do any wrong in my eyes until the day I came to Ryde and found her sleeping with Bruno. Something in my heart told me to come down here that day. Thankfully, I did, and the betrayal still stung to this very day.

"Camilla, you are no longer my problem. Call up my brother if you need help!" I bellowed.

"Antonio, wait," Camilla shouted through the phone. "It's about your deal with the gun runners."

Now she had my attention. How the hell did she know my latest business deals, let alone anything relating to business with the cartel?

"Camilla, meet me at my office in ten minutes. If you're not here within that time, prepare your funeral arrangements."

I hung the phone up before she could say anything else. I flung all the paperwork off my desk.

"Fucckkk!" I screamed.

Carlo rushed into my office with his gun drawn from all the screaming.

"Tony, what the hell?"

Carlo put his gun away after seeing everything was fine.

I slumped back down in my seat. I scrubbed my hand down my face in frustration. Sabrina hadn't called, Bruno was stressing me out, and my father was driving me crazy with the cartel.

Carlo walked over and handed me a glass of scotch.

"You seem like you need the whole bottle," Carlo said.

"Camilla's on her way."

Before he had a chance to reply, I held my hand up, interrupting him.

"She knows about the gun deal."

Thoughts filled my head, knowing the only way she'd know anything about it was through my brother. Once again, he had betrayed me. Suddenly, we heard a knock at the door. Camilla walked in, and I looked at her appearance. Her face showed hints that she had been crying. Her nose was red, and she had dark circles under her eyes. Her clothes hung off her slim body. At one point, her body was the only thing that could make me feel either good or bad. Having her in my life made things right. Now, I couldn't stand to look at her.

"Please sit…" I suggested.

"Baby," Camilla whimpered, trying to touch my hand, and I jerked back.

I interrupted her before she even started.

"I'm not your baby. My name is Antonio De Luca."

She looked sad at my comment and pulled a tissue from her pocket to wipe the tears before they fell down her face.

"I'm sorry about everything. The deal was something I overheard."

"How did you overhear?"

I grabbed my phone off my desk, checking to see if Sabrina texted.

"I was hanging with some friends, and they went off to the bar. As I followed them, I walked past some guys talking," Camilla said.

"What club were you at?' I asked.

"I don't remember," Camilla replied.

She looked scared.

Showing her a smile, I slowly got up out of my chair and walked toward the front of my desk. I nodded at Carlo to leave. He got up and passed his gun to me. I shook my head, but he still pushed it into my hands.

"Camilla, I'm trying hard to be patient with you. Somehow, you're making it difficult."

Walking behind her and placing my hands on her shoulders, I slowly caressed her shoulders.

"Are you comfortable?" I asked.

"Yes," Camilla answered.

"Good, now tell me what club and what friends you were with when you heard about this so-called gun deal."

Sitting in the chair next to her, I turned my body toward her with direct eye contact and held the gun in my lap.

Noticing the gun, her eyes got big, and she tried to jump up. I grabbed her arm roughly and placed her back in the seat.

"I think you know where this is going."

"Antonio p…. please…. he'll kill me," she stammered.

"You either tell me the truth or die, no matter what I find out."

Her cries grew louder, and I rubbed her back gently, hoping to give her a little comfort.

"Bruno and I went out with some friends, and I didn't find out till later that it was a business deal. I think he's trying to take over the cartel."

"See, now was that so hard?"

I stood from my seat and buttoned my jacket. After grabbing the gun and placing it in my safe, I walked Camilla out and yelled for Carlo to come back in.

"We need to set up a meeting with the Russians and my father," I demanded.

"It's Bruno?" Carlo questioned.

Nodding my head in acknowledgement, I said, "I need time to sort some things out."

"You can't kill him, Tony," Carlo stated.

Carlo looked directly in my eye, hoping to sway my sympathy toward my brother.

"I promise that ultimately it's up to my father."

Locking up my office, we headed out to handle business. Getting into the passenger side of his car, I checked the time on my phone. It rang with Bruno's name flashing across.

"Speak of the devil," Carlo joked.

"Hello," I answered.

"Where are you?" Bruno asked.

"Minding my business and working,"

I heard rustling in the background.

Carlo looked over at me out the corner of his eye, asking who was on the phone.

I placed my hand over the receiver.

"Bruno," I whispered.

"I need you to come to the restaurant," Bruno demanded.

"Why?"

Knowing my passive-aggressive tone would piss him off more, I continued to agitate him.

"Listen, little brother, just because he made you the Don, that doesn't mean shit to me. Get your ass over here. This is family business unless you want to hand it over to someone more worthy."

"When I find someone, then I'll do just that."

Hanging up before he could respond, I placed my cell back in my pocket.

"Run me by Washington Finance," I told Carlo.

"Tony, you're not in the best mood right now to see her," Carlo said.

"My mood is fine actually," I answered.

"Says the guy who…" Carlo replied.

I cut him off before he went into one of his rants.

"Just go please; the last thing I need is you babysitting me."

"Don't say I didn't warn you when she curses you out for dropping in unannounced," Carlo said.

Thirty minutes later, we pulled into her office building. Carlo handed the keys to the valet.

Noticing the receptionist at her desk, I gestured to Carlo to distract her while I headed up.

"Stay and keep her busy for me," I said.

"This won't end well," Carlo warned.

"Coming from the same guy who gets just as possessive of his woman."

Leaving him at the front desk, I followed the crowd on the elevator.

"I'm heading to Sabrina Washington's office. What floor is she on?"

The young man looked at me strangely. "I'm no stalker; I just signed a contract with her and forgot the floor number her office is on from what the receptionist told me."

"She's on the twentieth floor,"

"Thanks."

I turned back around and faced forward. The elevator dinged, and he got off on the twentieth floor. I could feel my blood boiling. It was over ten hours since I'd seen, smelled, touched or kissed my black beauty. She better pray I didn't spank her in her office for ignoring me.

I got off the elevator and looked around. I noticed a receptionist desk and walked toward it.

# CHAPTER FIVE

## SABRINA & ANTONIO

**S**abrina

As Spencer and I sat in my office, working and reading over contracts, he noticed my cell phone vibrating. The noise caused him to panic. I could tell he thought I was dating someone. I glanced over at my phone, and a ton of text messages popped up. I wondered if I did the right thing by ignoring him. Last night wasn't my ideal date, but I liked how I felt in his presence.

"Are you going to answer that?" Spencer asked.

"No," I replied.

"Sabrina, I'm not sure what's going on. It could be an emergency. Shouldn't you answer back?" he insisted.

"It's nothing, I promise. Let's finish this. I need everything finalized before my trip."

I placed the intercom button on my desk phone and called Lisa into the office.

"Did you need something?" Lisa asked.

"Yes, can you get us the Peterson contract, last year's portfolio, and some breakfast, please? Is that okay with you, Spencer?" I asked.

"It's fine. Whatever you have, I'll take," he answered.

His statement kind of threw me off. Looking back at Lisa, I gave her our food order.

"Sure, no problem. Be right back," Lisa said as she walked out.

"Thanks and let me know when my father gets in as well."

Spencer got up to walk closer to me. He stood behind me and placed his arm on my chair. I moved my chair in closer, and his arm fell off. Not giving up, he placed it back on the chair. I decided to just let him be.

"Okay, check out this layout. We could refocus the strategy from last year to put them with about a fifteen percent increase."

"That may not work with George. He likes to hold onto every penny," I informed.

As we talked, my phone vibrated again. I turned it off, and we continued working.

**Antonio**

I walked toward the receptionist. She wasn't bad looking. She was a little too thin for me. Looking at her name-plate, I noticed that her name was Michelle.

"Michelle… it is Michelle, right?" I flirted with her just like last time.

I could have just barged in, but I needed to get Sabrina on my side.

"It is. I remember you; it's Antonio De Luca, right?" Michelle asked.

"Yes, it's tough to forget such a beautiful face as yours."

"Mr. De Luca, do you flirt with all the women you come in contact with?" Michelle asked.

"Only a few that have that special something," I told her with a devilish grin on my face.

"And what's that?" she asked.

I watched her pull out her dress to make her breasts look bigger. I slowly ran my eyes up and down her length. Her breasts weren't big; they were just small enough that I could see the imprint of her nipple. My flirting must be working, so I turned it up a notch.

"I'll have to show you sometime, but today, I need to see Spencer Jones. We had a meeting a few days ago, and I forgot to tell him something about my account," I said, playfully grabbing her hand and kissing her cheek. I leaned closer and whispered in her ear, inhaling her perfume.

*She needs to lay off that Mary Kay, Walgreens perfume,* I thought as I fought to keep my nose from wrinkling.

"Normally, you'd need an appointment, but I'll make an exception. Here, put this visitor badge on and head through those doors. It's the office right when you walk in. It's all the way in the back. Can't miss it."

"See, that's what makes you special."

Noticing her receptionist, I approached, glancing at her closed door. I was tempted to barge in and drag her out.

"I need to see her, now!" I demanded.

"Excuse me, who are you?" Lisa asked.

"I need to see Sabrina, now. So, I can either bust the door down, or you can escort me to her door. Before you try to call security, you should know that I'm a client. The amount of press that I can bring down won't only put you out of a job, but your grandchildren will be buried in debt."

Lisa had a look of disbelief on her face, she knew I must be someone important.

"What's your name?" Lisa asked.

"I'm Antonio De Luca."

Not wasting any more time, I walked into her office and saw Spencer standing behind her with his arms around her. She sat at her desk, laughing at something he whispered in her ear. Something came over me. I slammed the door and screamed out.

"What the fuck is this?" I shouted out.

They both looked up at the sound of the door slamming. Sabrina jumped up and tried to pull Spencer back from walking toward me.

Lisa came running into the office.

"I'm so sorry, Sabrina. He wouldn't listen when I said you shouldn't be disturbed," Lisa explained, flustered with her face flushed from running behind Antonio.

"It's okay, Lisa. Just hold my calls for the next five minutes. Spencer, will you give me a few minutes? I'll handle Mr. De Luca's concerns," Sabrina demanded.

"Are you sure? Maybe I should stay," Spencer argued.

I walked toward Spencer, and Sabrina stepped between us.

"I'll be fine. Please just give me a few minutes," Sabrina said.

"Fine, I'll be right outside this door," Spencer muttered.

He started to walk out.

"I suggest you give Miss Washington and myself an hour to finish our discussion," I insisted, never taking my eyes off Sabrina.

She stood with her arms folded across her chest, biting her bottom lip. Even though I was pissed at her right at this moment, I couldn't help but notice how beautiful she looked in her red pencil skirt. Hugging her thick, brown thighs, her breasts spilled out of the tight pink shirt she wore with two buttons open. This had my thoughts scrambled all over the place, wondering what they were doing with the door closed.

I started to speak, but she cut me off.

"Have you lost your damn mind? This is my place of business!" she yelled out.

"Why didn't you respond to my messages?" I asked, trying to stay calm.

"We have nothing to discuss. There was no reason for me to text you back," she replied.

"So, you admit you read my text messages?" I asked.

Sabrina walked closer to me, just inches from my face. I could smell the peppermint on her breath.

"I'm going to say this once, so please, listen carefully. I'm not having dinner with you; this is not happening. I have to work, so please leave me alone and stop texting me."

Ignoring her statement, I pulled her into my chest and sniffed her neck, kissing her cheek in the process. I could never get enough of her sweet scent.

"I suggest you wear something sexy. I'm picking you up from here for our date tonight. Tell the lover boy out there to keep his fucking hands off you," I demanded.

She pulled away from my hold and walked over to the window.

"This controlling and possessive shit may work on other girls, but not with me. I'm not going out with you, and that's final," she argued.

Walking up behind her, my dick automatically got hard just from her proximity.

"You feel that?" I questioned.

I placed my hand on her hips and squeezed.

As a way of response, she moaned out.

"Answer me, baby."

"Yessss…" she stuttered.

I slowly rubbed my hands up and down her shoulders, back, and thighs. Hearing her moans cry out had me ready to strip her bare and take her right on the desk. I softly rained kisses on her neck, cheek, and ear.

"Fuck, I missed you so much," I muttered to myself.

"I hate you," she muttered as I pinched her nipples through her blouse.

I chuckled lowly from her flustered state. "That's a first; at least let me give you a reason to hate me," I teased and tightened a grip around her waist.

"I can't do this with you, Antonio. It's too intense and crazy. Barging in here and cursing out Spencer."

Sabrina walked out of my embrace and sat back at her desk. Crossing her legs and smoothing her skirt down, she buttoned her entire shirt. Walking toward her desk, I grabbed her chair and turned it, facing me.

"I don't share, and he wants what I have."

"First off, that's ridiculous. We've only gone on one date. That hardly makes me yours!" she bellowed.

"Baby, you have no idea. How about I make it up to you tonight?" I asked.

"If I agree, will you then leave my office so I can work in peace?" Sabrina asked.

"Yes, under one condition," I baited.

"Has anyone ever told you that you're the most incorrigible man they've ever met?" she questioned.

"I get that a lot. I'll leave if you make sure Mr. Jones stays away from you."

"Antonio, that's crazy. We work together. Besides, I have my hands full with another idiotic man that won't take no for an answer. Plus, you can't tell me who I talk to or work with. From the sign outside, it reads Sabrina Washington, Vice President of Washington Finance."

**Sabrina**

Antonio had his arms crossed over his chest. He smiled like what I had just said didn't mean anything to him.

"What's so funny?" I asked.

"Sabrina, are you okay?" Spencer yelled from outside the door.

"I'm fine, Spencer. Give me a minute!" I shouted.

"We have a meeting with your dad. We need to go," Spencer demanded.

"I'll be out in a second," I answered.

Antonio grabbed my waist again.

"This is not over. We both want this, and you can't fight it. Don't ignore my calls or texts again. Next time, I'll have to punish you." Antonio kissed me on the forehead and started to walk toward the door. "You look beautiful by the way," he told me.

**Antonio**

Leaving her office, I noticed Spencer standing with the receptionist at her desk. I decided to let him live for the moment. Winking at them, I headed to the elevator and left her building. We had a meeting with a new gun runner. My father was already breathing down my back about the cartel moving more product.

Seeing Carlo and Janice standing at his car, I walked up to her and gave her a kiss on both cheeks.

"Janice, it's so good to see you again," I said.

"Hey, Tony, I heard you've been causing my girl some problems," Janice replied with a grin.

"Now, where did you hear that?" I asked, narrowing my eyes at Carlo.

He smirked back at me in amusement.

"I have connections. Anyway, continue breaking her down. Liz and I have tried to get her to open up and get over her ex. The girl is stubborn."

I hugged Janice and kissed her cheek once again. I left Carlo and gave them a little privacy. I opened the passenger door and sent another text to Sabrina.

**Antonio:** Be ready for me tonight and wear something with easy access.

I know her response wouldn't be good.

**Sabrina:** Fuck you.

I chuckled at her response.

**Antonio:** All you have to do is ask, Bella.

I exited my messages and turned my phone off.

Carlo got in on the driver's side and shut the door.

"Hot date tonight?" I asked.

"Something like that," he said. "Did everything work out with Sabrina?" he questioned.

"Of course, did you doubt me?" I asked.

Carlo pulled off, en route to our meeting at Little Italy.

"Something told me I'd probably have to bail you out. Since you didn't go all caveman on her, I guess everything worked out well."

"You should never doubt me, brother," I boasted.

# CHAPTER SIX

## ANTONIO

"*D*oes she know about the family?" Carlo asked.

"No, and she won't hear about it from anyone if I have anything to say about it. I can't run her off before I have a chance to explore this thing we have between us." I answered.

"Brother, listen, if you feel something for her, then you need to tell her before it's too late. Your father and Bruno will make sure she's informed."

"Shit, you're right. I'll handle it after our date. No matter what, she's a part of my life now."

We pulled up to the restaurant Little Italy. It was a small hole in the wall building, at least fifty years old and run by the cartel. The smell of real authentic Italian food could be smelled wafting from the kitchen. I was sure that my mom's famous spinach ravioli was served here.

We greeted the owner, Vinny Esposito.

"Boys, how are you doing? You don't come around anymore," he said.

We both hugged Vinny and followed him toward our normal table at the back.

"Vinny, you know how it is. We just opened Ryde, and another club is getting built out of the country," I told him.

He nodded in understanding. Carlo grabbed the menu, and I declined mine.

"Are you getting the usual?" the owner questioned.

"Actually, I have dinner plans already. We're meeting a client."

"Say no more. I'll get your water sent over, and when they get here, I'll check in with you."

Vinny grabbed my menu and walked off to grab our drinks.

"What do you know about this guy?" I asked.

"He's Bruno and Alfredo's contact."

I ran my hands down my face. Thinking of Bruno and Camilla brought up so much anger. I needed to get it under control before he got here.

As soon as I cleared my thoughts of him, Bruno walked in wearing his usual all-black tracksuit. He wore a huge gold chain around his neck with the letter B in diamonds hanging from it. Some people said we looked like twins. I had a more muscular build, and he was leaner. The client walked in with him, wearing a black suit that looked to be a Kenneth Cole, and white button-down with a black tie. On his feet, I could spot Louis Vuitton anywhere.

Thinking that my only brother had sabotaged me again had me itching to cut his throat. He was that jealous of me. I shook off thoughts of killing my brother until I confirmed the information.

Bruno walked up to me and shook my hand. He slapped hands with Carlo, and they sat.

"Tony, I told you about Dante Marino," Bruno said.

Nodding in agreement, I kept my face stern, to prevent him from reading me. The best advice my father ever gave me was to never give off the impression that you care because this business could eat you alive. Your wife was the only one allowed to have that because at the end of the day, you would need someone to take the pressure and listen to your troubles, so the life and responsibilities didn't consume you.

Dante extended his hand toward me. I looked at it, and he looked embarrassed. I wasn't sure what Bruno had told him. I ran this business, and no favors were to be handed out.

"Let's skip all the pleasantries and get right to what you came here for," I stated.

The waitress walked over with four glasses of water and a bottle of scotch. She placed everything on the table and pulled her notepad out to take our orders.

Before she got started, I interrupted her.

"Cass, we won't be long. These two gentlemen can order after we leave."

My brother looked at me, stunned. Carlo moved his hand toward his gun. Everyone knew Carlo was my right hand. There was no need for me to have a gun.

"Little brother, I brought this deal in. I suggest you get off your high horse or get out of that lovesick mood and focus on cartel business," Bruno bellowed.

Now, why did he have to bring up Sabrina?

Popping my knuckles, I eased closer to the table, folding my hands together. I looked directly at my brother, smiling at him. I knew I had everything he wanted. Being named the Don of De Luca Cartel, a beautiful woman, and running a legitimate business on the side.

"Bruno, you could bring our father and the cartel a hundred-million-dollar deal, and I still wouldn't sign off on it. You know what your problem is? Jealousy. Somehow, you got in your thick skull that we're competing, and for what, I can't tell you. I'm the Don of the cartel. I run this and multiple businesses. All you do is work for me. I suggest you continue doing what I say and leave the business dealings to Carlo and me," I informed.

Looking down at my watch, I saw that I needed to leave and get ready for my date with Sabrina.

"Dante, hit up Carlo with the details. This meeting is over, like my brother stated. I have a date with the future Donna, and no one will stop that from happening," I told them.

I looked him right in the eyes with a satisfied expression on my face.

I walked out, bumping into my brother. He smirked back at me. The old me knew he was planning something, and I needed to be ready.

Carlo jumped in the driver's seat.

"Are you ready for war with your brother?" he asked.

"The question is if he's ready for me."

Carlo pulled up to my house ten minutes later. I jumped out, heading inside.

"Tell Sabrina if she needs Janice tonight, don't bother because I plan on keeping her busy for a while!" Carlo yelled out.

I burst out laughing and watched him drive off. I walked inside and turned my alarm off. Looking at the time, I saw that I had about forty minutes to get dressed and meet Sabrina for dinner.

# CHAPTER SEVEN

## CARLO

*Two hours later.*

Janice wore a cream, off-the-shoulder dress, with her hair pulled into a high bun, and open-toed shoes, with very little makeup. She ended up matching the color of my suit.

"This is nice, Carlo," Janice said.

"Are you surprised?" I inquired.

"Of course, but to be completely honest with you, most of the guys I date only plan on taking me to Burger King or McDonald's."

"You're kidding, right?" I questioned.

She took a sip of her wine while shaking her head at my questions.

"Nope, I mean usually, I like it that way. No stress from relationships, and I get what I want at the end of the day."

"What is it that you get out of that arrangement?"

"Dick," Janice boasted.

We both burst out into laughter at her honesty.

"I like you, Janice," I announced.

"It's just the first date. Don't go falling in love so

quickly now. Usually, it's after the first date, I get the guy hooked," Janice told me with a cheeky grin.

"What do you do that gets the guy hooked?" I asked with an arched eyebrow.

"Mr. Russo, I can't tell you all my secrets," Janice teased.

She winked at me and took another sip of her wine. She was a breath of fresh air, and I could see myself being with her for a long time.

"Anyway, how was your day today?" she asked me.

"Great, actually. We planned another club opening, and Antonio almost went crazy over your girl."

"She's so stubborn. It's going to take time. Alex did a number on her."

The waitress walked over with our plates of food. Janice ordered chicken marsala with salad on the side. I ordered chicken and scallops.

"Do you guys need anything else?" the waitress asked.

I looked at Janice, and she shook her head no.

"Enjoy your meal, and I'll be back to check on you."

"Wowww! Oh my, this is amazing," she moaned out.

"I like the sound of that."

We stared into each other's eyes.

"Don't start what you can't finish, Carlo," Janice smirked.

I wiped both sides of my mouth with a napkin before answering her.

"You never have to worry about me not being able to back up my claims."

She dropped her fork, slid the chair back, stood, and grabbed my hand.

I left a hundred dollars on the table, and we walked toward the bathroom. Before we entered, I pulled her to the side.

"Are you sure about this?" I asked.

She pushed me up against the wall, unbuckled my belt, and grabbed my dick, stroking it in my pants in the process.

"Fuckkk… Janice," I hissed.

*This can't be happening right now. I need to get her back to my place.*

"I can't do this here," I thought aloud.

Janice removed her hand, looking at me with a surprised expression on her face.

"Are you serious right now?" Janice furrowed her brows in annoyance.

I buckled up my pants and gathered my thoughts.

"I'm not like those other guys. I don't just want you for one thing."

We both walked back over to the table and grabbed our jackets that we had forgotten.

I held the door open for her, and we walked out of the restaurant. Turning her around to face me, I kissed her on the lips, cheek, and neck. I wanted to let her know she meant more to me than a one-night stand.

"What are you thinking?" I questioned as we drove away from the restaurant.

"I think this is too good to be true," she answered.

"Just think about what I said. I know about your past, and it doesn't mean anything to me."

"What do you mean you know about my past?" Janice asked with an arched eyebrow.

"Whenever anyone comes into our circle, we do a background check on them."

"What the fuck? How dare you spy on me?"

She turned her body toward the window and crossed her legs, tapping her foot impatiently. She looked cute while throwing a tantrum. I placed my hand on her hip to try to calm her down. She smacked my hand away.

"You don't get to touch me," Janice told me.

I rolled my eyes at her statement.

"Girl, you belong to me, and that means I can touch you whenever I want," I spat.

"Papi, you picked the wrong black bitch if you think you're running me!" Janice argued.

"We'll see about that," I mumbled under my breath.

"What was that?" she asked.

"Nothing," I muttered under my breath.

We pulled up to her apartment a few minutes later, and I started to open my door. She stopped me before I got out.

"Carlo, I'm not a little flower that needs saving if that's what you're thinking. I'm not ashamed of my past," Janice argued.

I leaned in and kissed her lips. They felt soft like two little plush pillows.

"You belong to me, the good, bad, and crazy," I demanded.

We both laughed at my statement. I got out of my car and walked around to open the door for her. Taking her by the hand, we walked up to her apartment, and I waited for her to get the keys out.

"Are you coming inside?" Janice asked.

"No, I have some things to take care of before meeting up with Antonio."

"Isn't he on a date with Sabrina?" Janice inquired.

I had to place my hands in my pockets to keep from taking her inside her apartment and fucking her brains out. I closed my eyes to calm the raging need to slide into her pussy.

"Carlo, hello… Carlo," Janice shouted.

"Sorry, what did you say?" I asked.

"Nothing, I'll see you later."

Noticing the disappointment on her face, I stopped her from closing the door in my face.

"Listen, I just need to handle some business. I'll stop by after if it's not too late," I said.

I caressed her cheek gently and looked into her eyes, so she didn't doubt that I was hot for her. A few minutes passed by, and she released a breath of air that she held onto from doubt. Placing a kiss on her forehead and watching as she closed the door, I walked to the car.

While driving over to Ryde, I received a text from Camilla.

**Camilla:** Meet me ASAP.

**Carlo:** I'm heading to Ryde.

*I hope she wasn't on any bullshit, because Janice looked like the type to shoot first and ask questions last if she found me with another woman, I thought to myself.*

# CHAPTER EIGHT

## SABRINA & ANTONIO

**S**abrina

"Hello, Miss Washington. I'm Salvatore, Antonio's driver," he stated.

"Hi, I'm sorry you came all the way out here, but I can drive my car," I told him.

"Mr. De Luca would be distraught if I didn't have you brought to him by a driver, specifically me," he said.

"I don't mean to sound so blunt, but I don't know you," I muttered.

"I'm his driver and have been since he was a little boy. I'd hate to lose my job."

He noticed that I wasn't buying his story. I watched as he pulled his phone out.

"Who are you calling?" I asked.

"Sir, she refuses to get in the car with me," Salvatore told the caller.

Salvatore nodded in agreement.

She looked down at her watch in frustration.

Finally, Salvatore passed the phone to Sabrina.

"Mr. De Luca wants to speak with you."

I rolled my eyes at him for calling Antonio on me. I grabbed the phone. I could tell that the man noticed the change in my breathing.

"Yes. Mr. De Luca?" I said.

"I told you not to call me that unless I'm making love to you," he replied lowly.

"I'd rather not," I stated.

"That attitude needs a little adjusting," he suggested.

I scoffed at his statement.

"Whatever."

"Keep it up. Anyway, Salvatore is my driver. You're safe with him, I promise," he informed.

"I need to at least go to my place to change."

"No problem," Sal said.

"I live at…"

Before I could get it out, Salvatore inputted my address into the navigation system.

"Do I even want to know how you have my address?" I asked him.

"Mr. De Luca is a very important man. Everyone he has contact with has a background check done on them."

"This is insane. Is he always like this?" I grumbled.

"Actually, ma'am, you're the first."

"I don't know if I should be afraid or flattered."

"Flattered, ma'am. I've never seen him so over the moon about someone since…"

"Since who? I can call you Salvatore, right?" I asked

"Sal is fine," Salvatore informed me.

"And you can call me Sabrina."

I looked at Salvatore with a small smirk as we pulled up to my condo.

"I'll try to be fast, but if you can't wait, I can always take my car."

"I promised to have you at his home by eight thirty," Salvatore answered.

"Okay, would you like to come up for coffee at least? I feel bad you're sitting out here alone," I asked.

"I'll be fine. I need to make some calls, anyway," Salvatore answered.

"Sal, you have the worst job in the world. Give me a few minutes, and I'll be right out."

Salvatore waved to me as I headed inside. I went into my home and hit the answering machine.

"Hey, call me. We have a lot to talk about, especially that fine man of yours. I saw him at Washington Finance yesterday. Let's do lunch," Janice said.

I deleted the message and listened to the rest of them, as I got dressed.

"Hey, beautiful. I'm sorry for earlier today. I'll make it up to you. Do you have any idea how much you drive me crazy?" Antonio said.

I blushed as I listened to his message again. Twenty minutes later, I showered and changed into a skin-tight, long, fishtail-length, black dress with cutout shoulders. I pulled my hair into a ponytail with minimal makeup.

I started a group text with Janice and Liz about tonight's plan.

*Sabrina: Hey, guys, I have a date tonight with Antonio, again. I'll keep you posted.*

*Janice: A second date already? Mr. De Luca works fast. Don't forget about lunch.*

*Liz: I'm so excited. Don't forget the condoms.*

*Sabrina: Liz, nothing is going to happen tonight. I'll call tomorrow for lunch plans.*

As I continued to text with Janice and Liz in the limo, Antonio called Salvatore on his phone.

"Yes, sir, she's in the car. We're heading to you now. I

would say breathtaking is an understatement," Salvatore answered.

I slowly picked up my head, looked at Salvatore in the rearview mirror, and blushed from his comment.

"Thank you, Sal. That's very sweet of you to say," I told him.

"I only speak the truth, and you look breathtaking tonight, Sabrina. Mr. De Luca may not allow you around any of his friends," Salvatore said.

"What can you tell me about his family and friends?" I demanded.

"I've worked for the De Luca family for over thirty years. Carlo is his best friend, more like his brother, and you already know about Bruno De Luca."

"Yes, we've met. A few weeks ago, at Ryde. He's quite the charmer. Has Antonio always had a jealous streak?" I asked.

"I think you may have to talk to him about that. We've arrived," Salvatore informed.

Salvatore got out of the driver's side and walked to the passenger rear door to help me out of the limo. I looked in amazement at Antonio's home. It was about twenty thousand square feet with a water pond in the front yard. Walking inside, I noticed high ceilings, large doors with gold handles, and there had to be about five to six bedrooms. I assumed that there was possibly a study or library and enough room here to raise three or four kids. Shaking the thoughts of children out of my mind, I saw Antonio opening the other side at the same time as Salvatore.

### Antonio

We stared into each other's eyes, and it was as if the heat from our earlier encounter ignited itself again. I watched as Salvatore stepped back and turned to Sabrina to say goodbye.

I could tell that Sabrina was trying to look away from my eyes as they captivated her.

"Thank you for coming," I said.

"Did I have a choice?" she groaned out.

I closed the door as Sabrina walked inside. I placed my hands around her waist and guided her to the living room to sit. I walked over to the bar.

"You have a beautiful home," Sabrina said.

"Thanks. Would you like a glass of wine?" I asked.

"Yes, please."

"Here you go," I replied.

I sat beside Sabrina, continuing to stare into her eyes.

"Are you going to stare at me all night?" she asked.

"I have no choice."

"Why do you say that?"

"I can't believe you're real."

Sabrina smiled back at me and took a sip of wine.

"Are you always this forward with every woman you date?"

"I don't date, Sabrina," I informed her.

"What exactly do you do then?" Sabrina questioned.

"I fuck, they leave, and before you ask, I've never had a woman at my home. You're the first," I answered.

Sabrina's eyebrows rose in shock, and she gulped the rest of her wine.

"Why me?" Sabrina demanded.

"Why are you the first?" I questioned.

"Why am I here? We could have just fucked at a hotel, and I hope this isn't you just satisfying some fetish of sleeping with a black woman."

I took her glass out of her hand and stood, as the tension in the room burned hotter with me not answering her question. I walked to the bar and poured more wine for myself.

"I like you, and I know you like me. Stop thinking beyond that, and let's have dinner. I cooked all my favorites for you," I told her, extending my hand toward her to grab.

"You cook?" she asked.

I led her to the kitchen. I stopped suddenly and placed a kiss on her shoulder.

"Sabrina, you look beautiful tonight," I complimented her.

"Thank you, Antonio."

As I led Sabrina down the hall, I couldn't help the wide grin on my face.

The dining room table was lit by candlelight. A large vase of fresh flowers sat in the middle of the table with light, soft music playing in the background.

"Who taught you how to cook?" Sabrina inquired.

"I'm Italian... my mother, of course, and my grand-mother," I answered.

"Are your parents still together?"

I tensed up as the topic of my family came up.

"They've been married for thirty-five years. What about your parents?" I questioned.

"My parents are still together and have been about as long as yours, but you know that already because you've done a background check on me," Sabrina muttered, seem-ingly annoyed by my intrusion on her private life.

"I think it's time Salvatore retired," I thought aloud.

Sabrina laughed.

"Do I amuse you, baby?"

Sabrina stopped waving her hands and laughed.

"Are you laughing at me?" I inquired.

"I'm sorry, but you can't get mad at Sal," Sabrina replied.

"Excuse me, I didn't know you and Sal were on a first-name basis," I said.

Sabrina came down from her laughing fit.

"Let me get this straight. First, you're jealous of Spencer, and now, you're jealous of Salvatore for talking with me?" she questioned.

"I won't apologize for wanting to be the only one who always puts a smile on your face. I want to be the first and last thing you think about."

Sabrina stopped talking and stared at me as I kept talking.

"I like listening to you laugh," I admitted.

"I never asked you to apologize," she groaned out.

"So, what do I need to do to make you mine?"

She got up from her seat and stood in front of me. She ran her fingers down my right and left cheek. She placed kisses on each of my eyelids, then my lips.

"I can't promise I'll stop if you start, Sabrina. You need to be sure about this," I said.

"Let's just have tonight, okay?" she replied.

Sabrina placed a kiss on my left and right cheek. I got up from my seat and walked Sabrina down the hallway to my bedroom. In the large and spacious room, a bed sat up high off the ground with a black and gold headboard, and gold steel bar handles on each side. Also in the room were a canopied couch, a fireplace, and an open deck with another canopy couch. Three large paintings hung on the wall, one showcasing my nightclub and the other two of naked women.

**Sabrina**

He shut the door behind me and stared into my eyes. I

could tell he wanted to make sure I was comfortable with what was going to happen tonight.

Antonio walked over and slowly ran his hands down each of my arms. He placed kisses on each arm and then slowly walked behind me and trailed kisses down my left and right shoulder. At the same time, he unzipped my dress.

"Antonio, aghhh… mmmh." I mumbled under my breath.

"Let me do this my way, baby," he demanded.

"Please, don't tease me," I moaned.

"Baby, you taste so sweet. Your skin is so soft. Let me explore you."

He helped me out of my dress and walked me over to the bed. He guided me near the center, and then he took off his shirt, shoes, and pants, slowly.

Watching my reaction, I never lost eye contact with him. He had finally taken everything off, except his boxers, and then walked over to the edge of the bed and grabbed each of my ankles. He gently placed kisses up and down my legs and thighs. He worked from the inner to outer thigh, and up to my stomach, then my breasts and neck.

"Baby, I can't promise to control myself tonight. I need you too badly, and fuck, I can't even think straight," he said to me.

"Fuck me, Antonio. I don't care about being gentle; just please fuck me," I begged.

He kissed me and let out a low growl.

"I need to be inside you."

He moved away and grabbed a condom from his pants pocket.

I slowly trailed my hand up and down his chest and onto his thighs, drawing small circles. I took hold of his hard erection and moved my hand up and down his chest.

He slapped my hand away.

"Woman… you're going to be… the death… of me," he panted. "Baby, you are so wet. I can smell you. You are so ready for me, aren't you, Sabrina? Tell me what you want," he demanded.

"I want you inside me now!" I demanded.

I looked shocked to see that he was at least nine or ten inches and prayed he took his time. He slowly placed the tip of his dick inside me and pulled back out.

"Fuck, Antonio, stop teasing me," I screamed out.

"I'm trying my best, baby. I don't want to hurt you. I am trying to slow this down. Otherwise, I can't promise I'll be gentle," Antonio said.

Antonio continued to grind his dick up and down the opening of my pussy, not entering me. He was just teasing me.

"Uhh, God, please fuck me now!" I screamed out.

**Antonio**

I took that as a yes and slowly entered her while keeping my eyes on her face. I wanted to see her reaction. I moved with small thrusts in and out while trailing kisses up and down her throat, cheek, and shoulders.

"Fuck, Sabrina, you feel so good. Baby, you are so tight."

Holding her thighs firmly against her chest, I spread them wide open.

"So sweet! I have to fuck you harder," I groaned.

"Mr. De Luca, stop talking, start fucking," she told me.

I chuckled as I pumped harder and faster.

"This can't be real. Arrrggh… shit… Baby, touch yourself," I demanded.

Sabrina moved her hand down slowly to her left breast, kneading and enticing me with her dark-brown nipples. She then kissed and squeezed each breast as I picked up the pace.

"Is this what you want, Mr. De Luca?" she whispered sexily.

I continued pounding into her pussy and rolling my hips, keeping up with her as she attempted to meet my movements.

Sabrina let out a gasp. "Ohhh… God!" she screamed.

"Turn over and get on your knees!" I demanded aggressively.

Sabrina withered beneath me, teasing her ass in my face. I smacked her ass.

"Don't worry, baby. I'm going to fuck that little ass of yours very soon," I murmured.

"Don't make… promises you can't keep," Sabrina groaned.

I bent down and kissed each of her butt cheeks and squeezed them, thanking God for sending her into my life. I moved slowly and licked her pretty pink pussy from the back and bit each cheek. Hearing her moan out made me more than ready to be back inside her. I slowly entered her from behind. At the same time, moving one hand to rub her clit and kiss up and down her back.

"Baby, youuu… Fucckkk," Sabrina screamed.

"I won't last long. Damn, you feel so good, Bella," I said.

**Sabrina**

The slap of his balls on the back of my thighs drove me to the most intense climax of my life.

"Antonio… Uhhhhhh. I can't hold on!" I moaned aloud.

"Come for me, baby. Let me feel you," he growled in my ear.

He placed feather-soft kisses down my back as he hit me with slow strokes.

"Shit… Bella. I've never moaned with a woman before. You have a hold on me that I can't control."

"Ohh, God... Yes!" I screamed out, convulsing and trembling in his arms.

We both fell over onto the bed after we climaxed together. He still was inside me, and his weight on top of me only made me orgasm for a fourth time tonight.

"I'm not done with you yet," he growled.

Antonio stayed inside me and continued to rub my back and shoulders, calming our breathing.

He spoke softly in my ear, thinking I was already asleep.

"Stay with me, Sabrina," he mumbled.

I opened my eyes to the words he just said. I couldn't help but feel safe in his arms, and a part of me wanted to see if we could work. Another part of me felt that the damage from Alex would carry over, and I couldn't bear the thought of another heartbreak.

Deciding that it was best to leave now before the morning came, I tried to move out of his arms. Antonio pulled me back to his chest and held onto me tighter, while lightly placing kisses on my neck and shoulder blade. I knew that he could feel the tension in my body. After lying there a few more minutes, we slowly fell asleep.

***Seven hours later***

Opening my eyes from the weight of Antonio and feeling suffocated, I finally eased out of his arms and got dressed to leave without waking him. Thinking about the night I spent with him brought a smile to my face.

I went home and got ready for work knowing that this was a one-time thing because he wasn't the type to have a relationship.

### Antonio

Two hours later, I woke up with a hard-on and slowly ran my hand across the bed, looking for Sabrina. It was her warm body that I had fallen asleep in. Noticing she wasn't there, I called out to her.

"Bella!" I yelled out.

I looked over at the clock and grabbed my phone. I walked into the bathroom and down the stairs. There was no sign of her. I called Salvatore from the house phone.

"Where is she?" I asked.

"I drove her home. She said you were asleep and needed your rest," Sal told me.

"Shit, next time, wake me up. Pull the car around, and Sal, you take orders from me and only me," I demanded.

"Of course, Antonio," Salvatore answered.

I hung up and texted Sabrina to find out why she left.

**Antonio:** *Why did you leave?*

Sabrina didn't respond.

**Antonio:** *Where are you? Pick up the fucking phone.*

When there was still no response, I tried calling, but it went straight to voicemail.

**Antonio:** I'm not fucking playing with you, Sabrina. I growled over the phone and hung up.

# CHAPTER NINE

## ANTONIO

Five thirty p.m. came around, and I decided I'd had enough of her ignoring me. I drove over to her office. Thirty minutes later, after dealing with traffic and security, I barged into her office as Spencer was talking to her.

"What the fuck is this?" I shouted angrily.

"Spencer, will you give me a minute, please? We'll pick this up later," Sabrina said.

"I don't think I should leave you alone with him," Spencer said, nervously looking between Antonio's narrowed eyes, heaving chest, and flaring nostrils.

"I'll be fine. Go check on our flight," she asked.

"What flight? Answer my fucking question, Sabrina!" I shouted, moving in closer to her desk, and leaned over with my hands laying flat to keep from snatching her up and fucking the shit out of her for leaving me.

"Are you insane, barging into my office and making fucking demands?" she said.

"Why the fuck did you leave?" I questioned, in a calmer tone.

"I have a busy day today. I don't have time for this. We had a good time last night, but we should leave it at that," she explained.

"I'm getting fucking tired of this chasing bullshit and you not answering my texts or calls!" I argued.

Sabrina walked from around her desk, wearing red high heels with an open toe, showcasing her soft, smooth legs. Her tight, light-blue, sleeveless dress had her round, perky ass sitting up high. I could feel my blood boiling, wanting to touch and take in her office. She had her hair split down the middle in wavy curls, just enough away from her neck to accentuate her diamond earrings and necklace. Her perfume lingered in the air, reminding me of a sweet cinnamon smell. I could feel my skin heating up. A part of me wanted to snatch her up and fuck some sense into her, but another part wanted to just hold her in my arms. She got directly in my face.

"No one asked you to chase after me. So, I suggest you forget last night and find some other bimbo to warm your bed. That's your type, right? A girl who doesn't speak, just does what you say," Sabrina replied.

She stood with her hand positioned on her hip, leg cocked to the side with her upper lip turned into a frown. I watched as her chest rose and fell in frustration.

"This headstrong, bitch attitude normally is sexy, but it's pissing me off at this particular moment. Where the fuck are you flying off to with that Spencer asshole?" I argued.

"That's none of your fucking business. Whatever I fucking do with him has nothing to do with you," she answered.

"Guess I'm not surprised. You did have every guy in the club eyeing you the night we met. I guess I was the lucky one," I retorted.

"Get out of my office!" she screamed.

Sabrina walked over to her door and opened it for me to leave.

I fixed my jacket and smoothed out the wrinkles as I walked toward the door. I left little space between us and looked her straight in the eyes.

"With pleasure, Miss Washington," I answered.

# CHAPTER TEN

## SABRINA

I walked over to my desk, dropped my head into my hands, and cried. A few moments later, Lisa knocked on the door and entered my office.

"Can I get you anything?" Lisa asked.

"Please call Janice, and Liz… confirm lunch and hold all my calls. Check my flight. I should leave immediately after lunch," I stated.

***Two hours later.***

I walked into the upscale restaurant, Crossings, and noticed Liz and Janice already sitting.

"You look like shit. What happened?" Janice questioned.

"Don't start. Did you order already?" I said. The waitress came over with her usual dry martini. Liz and Janice looked at each other with a bewildered expression.

"Okay, start at the beginning and don't leave anything out," Liz said.

"I slept with him, that's what happened," I answered.

"Normally, that would leave you happy, relaxed, or if it was horrible, a little bit agitated. This is the look of someone who killed your cat," Janice joked.

"Janice, let her finish and keep the drinks coming," Liz suggested.

"Nothing happened. I slept with him, then left before he woke up, and he called me a whore."

Janice and Liz both spat out their drinks in shock from my announcement.

"Are you serious? I'll kick his ass," Janice grumbled. She started to get out of her seat.

"It doesn't matter. We had a one-night stand, and we moved on," I answered.

"I have Carlo's number. I'll find out," Janice replied.

"Please, leave it alone. I have no time for this bullshit," I told her.

"Janice, shut up. Sabrina, exactly what did he say? Start from last night," Liz demanded.

I knew I looked annoyed with Liz and Janice.

"We had dinner last night, we fucked, and this morning, I left," I answered.

"Okay, but what's wrong with that? When did he call you a whore?" Janice asked.

"He didn't exactly call me that," I muttered.

"How did this start?" Liz said.

"He was asleep and whispered, 'stay with me,' and I may have left without saying goodbye," I mumbled lowly.

"Damn, talk about a hit and run!" Janice shouted.

Liz smacked Janice in the arm. "Are you scared to have a relationship because of Alex?" Liz asked.

"See, this is why I didn't want to talk about this. Somehow, it always comes back to Alex," I groaned.

"I think you like him, but you're self-sabotaging," Liz stated.

"Listen. I'm not the best person for relationship advice. But I'm with Liz on this. Sabrina, you fucked up. I think he likes you. Before you say anything, don't even bring race into this," Janice explained.

I opened and closed my mouth in shock.

"I agree with Janice on this. Take this week to think about what you want but realize that he obviously has real feelings for you," Liz said.

"I fucked this up, didn't I?" I replied, upset with myself.

"Yes, but let's get down to the most important issue," Janice said.

Liz and I both looked at Janice, trying to understand where she was going with her statement.

"What about the size of his dick? How was the sex, bitch? Don't leave anything out," Janice said.

I keeled over in laughter.

"Janice, I'm not talking about my sex life with you or anyone else. I will say I was delighted and happy," I answered.

"Sabrina, you're no fun. I can tell you from personal experience, Carlo is working with eight inches of thickness," Janice boasted gleefully.

Liz and I laughed in amusement, and they paid for the check.

"When are you coming back from Philly?" Liz asked.

"A week from today. I have to close this deal and having distractions right now would be terrible," I answered.

"Just think what good it could be for you to finally meet someone who shows up for you without trying to impress your family," Liz replied.

I gave Liz and Janice a hug. We walked out of the restaurant toward our cars to leave in separate directions. Hours later, I was sitting in the airport in first class with Spencer, getting ready to fly out of town to Philadelphia. This meeting was another way to secure my family's business across the US. I looked down at my phone and saw no calls from Antonio. Deep down, I was disappointed that he hadn't tried to reach out since the explosive fight in my office.

# CHAPTER ELEVEN

## ANTONIO

*I* was drinking in my office when Carlo walked inside with Bruno.

"Why are you sitting in the dark drinking?" Carlo asked.

Bruno walked around and grabbed a drink from the bar.

"Yeah, little brother, share the alcohol," Bruno responded.

I got up to pour another glass.

"Leave me the fuck alone!" I yelled.

"Does this have anything to do with Sabrina?" Carlo asked.

"Sabrina, that black bitch?" Bruno muttered.

I balled my fists up and hit Bruno square in the face.

"Don't you ever call her that again? You're not even worth being in the same space as her!" I shouted.

Bruno got up and pushed me up against a wall. We tussled and fought. Fists flew back and forth. The trash can and chair fell over. Carlo pulled me off Bruno and pushed him out of my office.

"Bruno, walk it off, man," Carlo suggested.

Bruno wiped his bloody nose and straightened his shirt.

"First Camilla, now this Sabrina chick, and Pop thinks you can run the family? You have no fucking clue what this life is about. I'll forgive you this one time, little brother, but loyalty is number one in this family. So, figure your shit out because Pop needs you at the house tonight." Bruno chuckled as he walked out of the room.

I attempted to get out of Carlo's grasp. I shoved him off me and headed to the bathroom to clean up. I came back out and sat at my desk. Carlo closed the door behind Bruno and sat down in front of me.

"I don't know what happened, but Bruno is right. You can't keep letting some woman dictate your life. Get your shit together. We have a business to run," Carlo announced and looked down at his vibrating phone and smirked.

"I'll be out in half an hour," I said.

I looked at my phone, thinking about contacting Sabrina, remembering how the last conversation ended. I started to dial her number and ended up calling my father instead. The last time we spoke briefly, he said that he had something to talk with me about. Probably something dealing with our illegal business.

"Did you speak with Bruno?" Dad asked.

"I'm at the club tonight, Pops. Can we meet afterwards? I need to wrap some things up here; it's going to take a while," I answered.

"Don't keep me waiting long. This interruption of my business will end very badly for whoever is spying for the enemy, and if you can't get a handle on this, it looks weak to our enemies and our family. I won't be able to save you," Father said sternly.

"I didn't ask for this life or position in this family," I

replied.

My father laughed into the phone.

"Son, no one asks for this life; you're born into it, and my patience is running thin. Get over whatever is fucking with your head and get down here. We have a problem and if it's not solved peacefully, I can't control what other people within this family will do, which will draw more attention to your business and that girl of yours."

I went dead silent on the phone, ice streamed through my veins at the sound of Sabrina's name coming out of my father's mouth.

"Did you think I didn't know about Miss Sabrina Washington? I'll take your silence as confirmation," Father chastised. "Never underestimate me, son. I have eyes and ears everywhere. I haven't decided yet if she's a solution or a problem for this family," Dad implied.

"She's neither. It's nothing, and it's over," I replied.

"Good, then keep it that way, and we'll not discuss the matter again. I'll see you tonight," Father said.

I hung up the phone and changed clothes before entering the club. I took one sip of scotch, threw my phone against the wall, and walked out. I spotted Carlo and Bruno talking at the bar, and I walked up to them, extending my hand out for Bruno to shake.

"Brothers again?" I asked.

Carlo watched the gesture and nudged us both in the arm for acting like an ass back in my office. He called over some women for them to party with.

"Let's get a round of drinks on me and see what we can get into tonight."

All four of the girls gave the men a lap dance in the VIP area of the club. Bruno and Carlo laughed and joked around with the girls. I noticed Camilla walking in with some friends. Carlo excused himself to answer his phone.

# CHAPTER TWELVE

## CARLO

"Hey, babe. What's up?" I asked.

"Are you at the club tonight?" Janice questioned.

"Yep, are we meeting up later tonight?" I asked her.

"Of course, but first, I would love to dance with you," Janice answered.

"Where exactly are you?" I questioned.

"Standing outside, waiting in line with some very scary-looking bodyguards," Janice answered.

"Baby, why didn't you tell me you were coming down tonight?"

I muffled the phone and walked outside to find her. "I'm over here."

I hung up the phone, pulled Janice into my arms, and kissed her on the cheek.

"Looking good tonight, baby," I said.

"Thanks. How good, exactly?" Janice flirted, squeezing my ass.

"Too good for these people. How about we head over to my place and have a private party for two?" I suggested.

"I think that could be arranged. I wanted to hang here for a little bit and dance first though."

I escorted Janice inside, and we headed to the bar. Janice looked around and scanned the room, looking for Antonio.

"What would you like to drink?" I asked.

"I'll take whatever you're having," Janice answered distractedly.

"Someone's feeling frisky tonight." I pulled Janice into a kiss.

"Is Antonio here tonight?" Janice asked.

"Ouch, that hurts my feelings. Are you just using me to get into my brother's pants?" I questioned.

Janice smacked me on the arm and kissed me on the cheek.

"If you need something, I can get it for you. I'm also part owner of Ryde," I informed her.

"I know that, silly man. I just wanted to talk to him," Janice replied.

"Talk to him about what?" I questioned.

"Promise you won't get mad?" she said.

"Janice. What's going on?" I asked.

"Promise me first," Janice said.

"Fine, I promise."

"I had lunch with Sabrina today, and she told me they fought," Janice answered.

"That's explains what the drinking was about," I mumbled to myself.

"What drinking?" Janice asked.

"Shit, that idiot. I swear, he always gets into these situations with women, and I end up having to clean up after him," I muttered.

"What are you over there mumbling about?" Janice asked.

I looked around the room and caught Antonio talking with Camilla. Janice followed what I was looking at and attempted to confront him. She had no clue that when he was in a mood, it was best for everyone around to stay away from him.

"That bastard was just with my friend, and now he's hooking up with some other slut bucket," Janice shouted and tried to get out of my arms. I tightened my hold.

"Babe, leave it alone." I stroked her cheek and kissed her lips to calm her down.

"I hope you don't think you'll ever play me like that," Janice stated and pointed at my chest.

"I know my limitations, babe," I replied.

"Glad you figured that out because I'd hate to have visits," Janice replied and stood on her tippy toes to peck my lips.

"Visits? What do you mean visits?" I inquired.

"Boy, this hair doesn't do well in jail. If I caught you cheating, murder is the case they'd give me, and my hair stylist barely makes house calls," Janice joked and walked off heading toward the door and locking it with a teasing grin on her face.

# CHAPTER THIRTEEN

## SABRINA

$\mathcal{I}$ entered my hotel room and fell onto the bed from exhaustion. I turned my phone on and saw one missed call from my mom. I decided to jump into the shower before I called her back. Before entering the bathroom, a knock sounded on the door.

"Sabrina?" Spencer said.

"Who is it?" I asked.

"It's me," he answered.

"Hey, what's up?" I asked and opened the door slightly.

"Can I come inside?" he asked.

"I was actually about to take a shower and order room service," I replied.

"That's why I came up here. I was heading down to the restaurant and wanted to see if you wanted to join me?" he asked.

"I'm pretty tired. I just want to curl up and go over the research for this meeting tomorrow," I responded.

"Are you dating Antonio De Luca?" he blurted out.

"I'm not talking about my private life with you, Spencer," I told him.

"I guess that answers my question," Spencer answered in disbelief.

"I think we both had a long day, and I need a shower and some rest. I'll see you tomorrow, Spencer," I suggested.

Spencer looked around the hotel room, thinking of a way to prolong his stay.

I noticed his eyes roaming with thought. He finally left the room, and I called in my room service order. Twenty minutes later, I heard a knock on the door.

"You can place it over by the table in the corner."

I grabbed my purse off the couch to give him a tip. The waiter thanked me and left.

I undressed and walked into the bathroom to hop into the shower. Twenty minutes later, I walked out wrapped in a towel that covered my thick frame and out my boy shorts and a tank top from my suitcase. After rubbing lotion on my legs, I lay on the couch and ate my now-cold dinner. I called my mother before trying to sleep, but thoughts of the last few hours kept me awake. The same dream of being wrapped in Antonio's arms and him placing open-mouthed kisses along his jaw line and down his throat, kept flashing in my mind. I kept seeing visions of him rubbing up and down my thigh, as he tightened his hold around my waist and placed his hands on my ass and squeezed.

Suddenly, I ran my hand down my stomach and into my panties. Keeping my eyes closed, I pictured the way his nine inches of thick cock glided in and out of my pussy, causing me to moan out his name. Just thinking about him made me wet, and I dipped one, then two, and three fingers into my wet pussy, hitting my clit and causing my breathing to increase. My heart pounded faster.

Two orgasms and a second shower later, I finally passed out and slept like a baby.

Morning crept up fast. Spencer and I met down in the lobby for breakfast before our early morning meeting.

"Did you sleep well last night?" Spencer asked.

"I did actually. What about you?"

"It took awhile but after some drinks, I finally passed out."

I checked my phone as we waited for the waitress.

"Listen, about last night, I want to apologize," I said.

"Don't worry about it." Spencer reached over and grabbed my hand. "I know I tend to come on too strong sometimes; you can't blame a guy for trying. I mean, look at you."

I smacked Spencer's hand away in a playful motion.

"Spencer, we're friends. Don't worry about it. Let's just finish this meeting and hopefully get some new business while we're here."

Spencer and I walked into the hotel's conference room and greeted the owner and son of the Denver Rangers basketball team, Daniel Anderson Sr. and Daniel Anderson Jr. We've tried for the past two years to get the Denver Rangers' owner to invest with Washington Finance, and we finally landed a meeting.

"Well, aren't you a lovely sight to see," Daniel Sr. said, shaking my hand firmly.

"Hello, Mr. Anderson. Thanks for agreeing to a meeting."

"Anything for you sweetheart. So, tell me how you're going to make me even richer."

"Nice to see you as well Daniel Jr. How's Mariah doing?"

"Actually, we're expecting again. She's home taking care of the little ones."

"Shall we get started, gentlemen?"

Spencer escorted everyone over to the conference table with everything all set up for our meeting.

After finishing the meeting, we headed back home to New York. As we walked out of the airport toward a chauffeured car holding a sign for Washington Finance, I bumped into a guy.

"Ohhh...shit!"

My purse and phone fell to the ground.

"Damn. Sorry, Miss," he said.

The stranger and I bumped heads as we attempted to pick up my purse and phone.

"Damnit," I cursed.

He grabbed me by the elbow to keep me from falling.

Spencer walked up after grabbing his luggage and tried to stake a claim on me by wrapping his arm around my waist and pulling me into his chest.

"Sorry, didn't mean to step on your toes," the man apologized.

"Sabrina, you okay?" Spencer asked.

I moved out of Spencer's hold and took my phone and purse out of the man's hand.

"I'm fine, thanks."

"Didn't mean to run into you like that, beautiful," the stranger said.

"I'm fine. Thanks for grabbing my stuff," I answered.

"It was my pleasure, Miss?" he inquired my name.

"Sabrina Washington."

I extended my hand out to shake his, and he grabbed it and covered it with both hands.

"Derrick, Derrick Smith, and it was nice running into you, Sabrina."

We smiled, and I pulled my hand away. I turned to open the door as the driver and the stranger attempted to open it at the same time. Spencer walked around to the other side and started to get in on the other side, mumbling under his breath in anger.

"You didn't have to do that," I said.

"I did," Derrick replied.

He closed the door, and I rolled down the window.

"My mom would kill me if she found out I didn't open a door for a beautiful woman," he replied.

"Well, thank you again," I smiled.

He smiled back, and the driver pulled off as we watched each other until he faded out of sight.

"Don't you think you have enough going on with that thug De Luca before moving on to the next guy?" Spencer suggested somewhat snarkily.

"Spencer, get over it," I argued.

Finally arriving home, I got out of the car and grabbed my suitcase from the trunk with the chauffer's help. I tipped him and walked toward my building. Spencer got out of the car to stop me before I headed in.

"Sabrina… Sabrina, wait, please…" Spencer begged.

I turned around and looked at Spencer in sympathy.

He ran his hand down his face in agitation.

"I'm tired and hungry. Can we do this another time?" I suggested.

"I just want a chance," Spencer said.

I rolled my eyes in annoyance.

"Why?" I asked.

"Why what?" Spencer questioned.

"Why do you want to date me?" I asked.

"Sabrina, our families work together in the business world. We've been family friends for a long time. We briefly dated in college…"

I stopped him before he continued.

"Spencer, we hung out a few times in college, I don't call that dating, and we both agreed friendship was better for us. We want different things out of life, and I'm sorry, but the chemistry isn't there."

I turned around and walked toward my building, leaving Spencer outside. Turning the lock on my door, I walked inside and dropped the keys on the counter. Placing my purse and phone down, I pulled my shoes off and plopped down on the couch in exhaustion.

"What am I doing?"

My phone rang, and my sister's name flashed across the screen.

"Hey, sis," I said.

"Hey, boo," Ashley said.

"I'm shocked. You're calling me from work?" I asked.

Ashley giggled.

"I know, right? The life of a surgeon never stops. How are you doing?" I yawned into the phone. "Talk to me, sis. You sound out of it," Ashley said.

"Just normal problems: work, Alex, Spencer, and Antonio."

I mumbled Antonio's name.

"Okay, I get Spencer, fuck Alex, and who the hell is Antonio? He sounds like a bad boy," Ashley said.

"Shit, he is, and that's the problem. The asshole is fine, sexy, dominating, possessive, and sweet all rolled into one," I explained.

"Someone sounds like they're in love." Ashley chuckled.

"Girl, bye."

"This sounds like a sister sleepover discussion," Ashley said.

"That would be fun. Let me call Janice and Liz," I announced.

"Awesome. Hit me up later with the details."

After ending my call with Ashley, I got up from the couch and walked into the kitchen. I checked the fridge for any leftovers and chose to heat up some meatloaf. As I moved around in the kitchen, someone knocked at the door. I looked over at the time on the microwave's display. It read nine p.m. and wondered who could be coming by at that hour. Opening the door without looking through the peephole, I attempted to shut it in his face.

"Sabrina, baby, wait!" Alex yelled.

Alex stopped the door from shutting with his foot. I tried to put all my weight on the door. I gave up after a few minutes.

"Alex, leave me alone!" I shouted.

"No, just listen to me first," Alex begged.

Holding the door open and watching the neighbors walk by, I decided to let him come inside.

"Fine, you have five minutes."

"Baby, you know anything I do takes more than five minutes," Alex joked.

"Keep telling yourself that lie, and maybe one day you'll believe it."

Sitting on my couch and picking up the latest Essence magazine. Alex followed me and pulled it from my hands.

"Sorry, I..."

My phone ringing interrupted him. I picked it up and noticed Janice calling.

"I need to take this. Hold on."

"Hello..." I said.

"Girl, when did you get home?" Janice asked.

I walked to the kitchen to keep Janice from hearing Alex talking.

"A few minutes ago. Are you coming over tonight with Ashley and Liz?" I asked.

"You already know. I'm bringing the martinis and porn," Janice joked.

"Girl, you have no good sense."

Alex walked into the kitchen, and I placed my finger against my lips to tell him not to talk. He arched an eyebrow in disbelief of me hiding him from whoever I was on the phone with.

"Listen, I'm just checking on you. I saw your boy tonight," Janice told me.

"Who?" I asked.

"Honey, if you have that many that you can't keep up with them, then send one over to Momma Janice," she joked.

"Doubt Carlo will let you have a toy on the side," I replied.

"Girl, Carlo don't run nothing over here," Janice said.

Suddenly, Sabrina heard rustling noise on Janice's side of the phone.

"Stop playing Carlo and give me back my phone!" Janice screamed.

"Shut up before I spank you!" Carlo yelled.

I burst out in laughter at Janice and Carlo arguing.

"You don't run me. Shit, you better call up your other whores!" Janice shouted.

"You're right, I sure will," Carlo said.

I listened to Carlo dialing a number, knowing that he was pretending to call someone. I heard Janice in the background wrestling with Carlo for the phone.

"Boy, don't play with me. Try me if you want to!" Janice shouted.

"Hey baby, come on. The old ball and chain is leaving for the night," Carlo joked.

"Carlo, you are too much," I said.

"She's leaving right now," Carlo said.

"Where's my gun at?" Janice questioned.

"Shoot me, and I'll shoot you back. Here, take your damn phone." Carlo handed the phone back over to Janice.

"Hello, bitch, he's taken!" Janice yelled.

"Janice, it's me, Sabrina." I laughed.

"Sabrina, ohh… Damn, sorry, girl. I swear Carlo's going to make me snap on his ass one day. He plays too much," Janice announced.

I heard Carlo slap her on the ass.

"Stop, Carlo. You know that's my spot," Janice said.

"Okay, you horndogs. That's my cue to go. I'll see you tonight," I said.

I hung up and looked at Alex as he stood across from me in the kitchen.

"How's Janice?" Alex asked.

"Let's not pretend like you care."

Alex walked close to me, and I placed my hand on his chest to push him back.

"Anyone you love means something to me as well, baby," Alex explained.

I felt agitated and overwhelmed.

"Alex, just tell me why you're here?" I questioned.

Alex sighed, turning away from me, and walked into the living room. I followed him, and we sat on the couch. I moved a few feet away to give us space.

"I still love you," Alex confessed.

"Okay," I answered.

"Do you still love me?" Alex asked.

"No, and before you get started with whatever story you have as an excuse, save it. You hurt me to the core. Not a little hurt, as if you damaged my car, or messed up and washed my reds with white clothes. You slept with another woman and got her pregnant. Then, you proposed to her after proposing to me. Did you think I'd never find out?"

Alex lowered his head in shame.

"Sabrina, it was the biggest mistake of my life, and I wish I could take all of it back."

"I'm sorry, but it's too late."

I stood and walked toward the door. After a few minutes, Alex followed me.

"I don't love her, and I broke it off with her. We can start over," Alex pleaded.

"And the baby?" I questioned.

"I'm not sure it's my baby."

"Excuse me, did you just say you don't know if it's your baby?" I asked

"Bri Bri…"

I chuckled in amusement.

"So, let me get this straight. You cheat on me and propose to her, thinking she's pregnant with your child, and she possibly cheated on you as well?"

"I know it'll take time for you to work through this," he said.

"I don't need any more time. We're done; lose my number," I answered.

"What?" he said.

I pushed Alex out of my apartment.

"Tell Sharon that payback is a bitch."

I slammed the door and walked back into the kitchen. Gathering the cookware to check on my food in the oven, I continued with my night of solitude, blocking Alex's surprise visit out of my mind.

# CHAPTER FOURTEEN

## ANTONIO

"What can I do for you? It's Liz, right?" I said.

"I won't take up too much of your time. May I sit?" Liz asked.

I gestured for her to take a seat.

"I know you're a busy man. I wanted to talk with you about Sabrina," Liz asked.

"Did she send you here?" I questioned.

"Actually, she just got back from out of town and has no clue I'm even here," Liz informed me.

"I see. Would you like a drink?" I asked.

"I'm fine. Listen, I just wanted to say that she's scared, and whatever happened between you two freaked her out. She tends to meet a lot of guys who don't hang around for long," Liz said.

"And you're telling me this, why?" I questioned.

"I know you like her, and for someone to bust not once, but twice, into her office and kick Spencer Jones around is pretty special in my book."

I grinned, thinking back to that day.

"I'm not sure what Sabrina has told you, but nothing is going on between us," I said.

Liz stood and grabbed her purse.

"Sabrina's a big girl. She's tough, sweet, loyal, and loves with all her heart. She's been hurt badly in the past, so you have to continue breaking down that wall around her heart. It won't be easy, but she's worth it," Liz replied.

"Thanks for the advice, but it was a one-time thing," I said.

"Whatever you say. She's back home from her business trip. If you change your mind, I wouldn't call. Show up at her front door instead. She may hate you right now, but she loves the chase."

Liz walked out of my office. I took a sip of my scotch and thought about what Liz said.

I walked out to Salvatore holding the door open to my car after I finished at the club. I was heading to my parents' home for a late-night meeting. The car pulled up to the compound, and I spotted heavy bodyguards and increased security.

"Where's Mama?" I asked.

"She's sleeping. Let's go into the office," Father answered.

"Can we make this quick? I have a lot of work to do tonight," I asked.

"If that work has to do with the rat, then fine. If not, it can wait. Sit down and look at this."

We walked into the office. I sat in the chair in front of my father's desk and picked up a pile of surveillance photos.

"What am I looking for?" I asked.

"That's your job. I have over twenty photos of this piece of shit coming in and out of De Luca's coffee warehouses. I've had my contacts look up everything on this guy, but nothing is confirmed. I need you to work with Bruno and your uncle to get this contained," my father said and took a sip of his scotch.

"How do you want it contained?" I questioned.

"I want them killed, but first, find out what they know about the family," Father suggested.

"I told you before, I'm not into the whole killing aspect of the cartel," I told him. "I'll help find out who this is, but I'm not killing anymore."

My dad laughed as I spoke.

"I told your mother she babied you too much, made you soft. How do you think you got where you are, son, huh? Did you think you just happened to fall into being a successful owner of so many clubs? Are you that naïve or just stupid?" Dad shouted angrily.

I started to speak, and my dad slammed his hand on the desk.

"Silence! I will not be disrespected in my home. Unclench your fists!"

He came from around his desk and got in my face. "Don't mistake my love for you, son. This will be done with or without your assistance. This is what happens when you become a part of this family. We have a deal, or have you forgotten? I stay out of your personal life, and you take on more responsibility. Are we clear?" my father insisted.

"I haven't forgotten our deal, and a part of that means I make the decisions on what happens under my orders. So, unless you decide to make Bruno the head of this family, then I still have the final say," I suggested.

I walked out on my father. I could tell he was proud of the assertive stance I was taking.

"Tell Ma I'll see her for Sunday dinner!" I shouted as I

pulled the front door open and made my way back to the car.

* * *

I MADE it back home and undressed for bed. I glanced down and saw Sabrina's earring laying on the ground. I picked it up and placed it on the dresser, then jumped in the shower.

Fifteen minutes later, I crawled into bed, hoping to dream about her. After I had been asleep for an hour, my phone vibrated.

"Fuck… my life," I groaned. "Speak."

"Boss, she's at home, and it looks like she has some company," my bodyguard informed me.

"Who is it?" I demanded.

"Not sure. I just see her light on and hear music playing," he explained.

"If you see a man leave, bring him to the warehouse and call me," I replied.

"What do we do with her if she sees us?" he asked.

"Kidnap her and bring her to me," I instructed.

I hung up the phone and went back to sleep.

* * *

I HAD an early morning flight and business meetings with Carlo scheduled for the day. I met him at the airport.

"Someone didn't get any sleep last night," Carlo joked.

"Fuck off." I pushed Carlo out of my way and climbed into the awaiting limo.

"What's the matter, princess? You didn't get your late-night treat?" Carlo laughed at me, putting his middle finger up at me.

"I had a visitor come to Little Italy during my meeting with the Russians," I said.

"Who?" Carlo asked.

"Sabrina's friend," I said.

"Janice was with me last night after her attempt at joining Sabrina's sleepover didn't go too well," he said.

"Why didn't it go well?" I asked.

"She was missing this dick," Carlo smirked.

"At least one of us got some last night. If I don't get laid soon, my balls are going to turn blue from being clogged up," I joked.

# CHAPTER FIFTEEN

## CAMILLA

This bitch thought she was going to get my man. Soon, my plan would work, and I would be back on top with my man and his money. I refused to let him be happy with her. I made a mistake with Bruno. This wasn't over. I drove to her apartment after watching Sabrina have lunch with her friends. As I drove back home, my phone rang.

"Hey, baby," I answered.

"Sweetheart, did you do as I asked?" Alfredo asked.

"Of course I did. Carlo thinks it's Bruno, and pretty soon, Antonio will be convinced too," I boasted.

"Good… Good. We have to step it up with plan B. I need Antonio out of the picture so we can get our hands on the cartel," Alfredo informed me.

I was annoyed with dealing with Alfredo, but I had no other choice. Bruno would never betray his family, besides sleeping with me. That was only done because I drugged him, and Antonio just happened to catch us by accident. The goal was to blackmail him. In the end, everything was coming along nicely.

"Well, things on my end are good. Bruno could be a problem though. I have Carlo's ear, and you know he can get Antonio to agree to anything. All we need is to have Bruno taken out, I marry Antonio, and you kill him, making me a widow."

"In due time, sweetheart. My brother is giving that little shit my business," Alfredo grumbled.

I pretended to get interrupted by another call.

"Babe, I have to go. Someone is beeping in..." I told him.

"Don't forget to get that black bitch out of Antonio's life," Alfredo demanded.

"I'm working on it. Just hold up your end of the deal," I replied.

"Am I seeing you tonight?" Alfredo asked.

"Like usual. I'll be at the hotel around midnight. I need to make sure Antonio doesn't have a detail on me," I told him.

We hung up, and I smiled evilly from my plan to use everyone to get my family's money back. If the De Lucas had never stolen from my father, he wouldn't be in debt to the cartel. I loved Antonio, but when he broke up with me after I cheated, the love went away. My goal was all about getting even to destroy the De Luca family, and that included his little black beauty, Sabrina Washington.

"They'll never know what hit them." I smirked.

# CHAPTER SIXTEEN

## SABRINA

Longing to see, hear, and touch him had left me in a state of denial. I refused the temptation of calling and seeing how he was doing. After the last encounter at my office, I had decided to move on officially from Antonio De Luca. While working in my office, Janice walked inside without knocking and sat in the chair in front of my desk.

"What?" I asked.

Janice stared at me with an amused look.

"Are you just going to sit and watch me like a bug under glass?" I asked.

Still not answering me, Janice kicked up her feet on my desk.

"Okay, I see what game you're playing. What did I do?" I groaned out in frustration.

"I'm glad you asked," Janice replied.

I rolled my eyes at her in annoyance.

"I don't have time for your opinion on my love life," I said.

"Bitch, it's me you're talking to. Not Liz, Antonio,

Ashley, or Alex. Me, Janice, your best friend. The one who stayed up with you all night after finding out Alex cheated on you and suggested we break into his apartment to kick his ass. Also, the best friend who helped you when you had your miscarriage. So, please, don't sit up here and tell me you don't have time for my opinion. Oh, honey, you got this chick all the way twisted if you think I'm going to keep quiet," Janice said.

Janice got out of her seat and walked over to the couch. She waved to me to walk over and have a seat next to her.

"Come on, it's time for 'Dr. Janice' hour, tell her all your problems, and she'll get to the root cause and get you right in no time," Janice said boisterously.

Janice picked up a pencil and pad.

"Are you seriously going to take notes like a real therapist?" I asked.

"Yep, bitch. You got issues. It's causing me not to get dick, so I need you to sit and tell me the problems."

Janice walked over to me, grabbed me by the elbow, and escorted me to the couch. Blowing out a breath of frustration, I sat on the couch.

"I can't stand you," I stated.

"Well, join the club," Janice gloated.

As I started to talk, Lisa knocked on my door.

"Come in," we said at the same time.

"Your two-thirty appointment is here. Derrick Smith, and I must say, you lucked out. He's so hot," Lisa whispered.

Derrick walked in right behind Lisa as she talked. I was surprised when he realized that he was making eye contact with the same woman from the airport.

I jumped up from my seat and fixed my clothes and hair.

"Damn," Janice muttered loudly as she boldly looked him up and down.

"Janice, really?" I chastised.

Lisa looked at me, Janice, and Derrick, feeling the tension in the air. She walked out amused at my flustered state.

"I didn't think I'd see you again," Derrick said.

Derrick walked up to me, invading my space and caressing my cheek. Janice cleared her throat, hoping to cut the sexual tension in the room.

"Uhmmm… Okay. I think that's my cue to go. Sabrina, we'll talk later," Janice suggested.

I just nodded in agreement, not even thinking of what Janice just said. I was too overwhelmed with being in Derrick's presence again.

"Let me take you out tonight?" Derrick asked.

"How did you find me?" I inquired.

"After our little run in New York, I noticed your business card had fallen out of your purse at the airport. I asked around about you, and here I am. Hopefully, you don't think I'm a stalker."

"Well, that's debatable, but okay," I replied.

Derrick smiled at my quick response.

"You're still the most beautiful woman I've ever seen," Derrick said.

Spencer walked inside without knocking and interrupted our moment.

"Sabrina, we need to talk," Spencer demanded.

I looked away from Derrick toward Spencer and removed myself from Derrick's embrace.

"Umm, Spencer, can this wait? I have a meeting with… I'm sorry I didn't get your last name," I said, breathlessly.

"Smith. Derrick Smith," Derrick replied.

Spencer walked back over to the door and held it open

for Derrick to leave. Derrick looked over at Spencer and smirked in amusement at his jealousy. Derrick glanced over his shoulder, staring at me as he walked out.

"I'll get your number from your receptionist. Look for my call later."

"I look forward to your call." I giggled.

After Derrick left, I turned toward Spencer, interrupting him before he started talking.

"Leave. I'm not in the mood for you and your tantrum. How dare you interrupt a meeting I had scheduled," I forced out.

"Sabrina, please, just listen to me. I did a little investigation on that Antonio character. He's dangerous," Spencer said, agitatedly.

"I don't care. Anything relating to Antonio De Luca is no longer my business. This is a professional environment, and I suggest you act like it and leave my love life alone."

I walked off and grabbed my purse and coat. I stood next to the door and waited for Spencer to follow me out of my office.

"We're not finished with this conversation," Spencer muttered.

"I am. You can do whatever you want. Good night, Lisa. I'll probably be in late tomorrow," I informed her.

Lisa smiled and giggled at the frown on Spencer's face.

"What's so funny?" Spencer asked angrily.

"Ignore him. Why don't you take the rest of the day off. Pick up early tomorrow," I said.

I walked off to the elevator, and Spencer huffed and stormed off to his office.

* * *

After ignoring Antonio's phone calls and text messages and dodging him at work for the last week, I was out on a date with Derrick.

"You look beautiful tonight," Derrick said.

"Thanks. You look handsome as well," I replied excitedly.

"After you dodged me the last three times, I'm glad you finally took me up on my offer to have dinner," Derrick replied sadly.

I took a sip of my wine to avoid the conversation. I didn't want to get Derrick involved with my situation while I was dealing with Antonio. He seemed like a stable guy and having to deal with feelings getting between us was the last thing I needed. Still dealing with my questionable situation with Antonio was hard enough.

"I know he hurt you, but you can let your guard down with me," Derrick suggested.

"Sorry about that. It's just complicated," I said, deep in thought.

Derrick grasped my hand and kissed it. I smiled and looked into his lovely hazel-brown eyes. I watched as Antonio and two of his bodyguards walked toward my table. I knew I had a terrified look on my face as he approached. I pulled my hand away from Derrick.

"What's wrong?" Derrick asked.

"Get up," Antonio demanded angrily.

Antonio kept his eyes on me, waiting for me to disagree. I could tell he was done being patient with me.

"I'm not going anywhere with you," I replied nervously.

Derrick looked between Antonio, me, and the men standing around our table.

"I suggest you get up and walk out of here with me, or I could drag you out of here over my shoulder. The choice is entirely yours," Antonio said.

"I think the young lady gave you an answer. Now, if you can excuse us, we'd like to get back to our date," Derrick spat.

It was obvious he was rubbing it in that he was out with me.

My eyes grew big at his aggressiveness toward Antonio.

Antonio turned his attention toward Derrick. He pulled me out of my seat. He sat in the chair that I had just vacated and pulled me down onto his lap. Everyone in the restaurant looked shocked by his boldness. I tried to get out of his arms. He only tightened his hold. He pulled my chin toward his face and placed a soft kiss on my lips in front of Derrick. Derrick and I both looked surprised.

"You may be on a date, but not with this one. She belongs to me." Antonio smiled at Derrick wickedly.

He patted me on the butt, and I got up. After he grabbed my coat and purse, I took them out of his hands, pleading with Derrick through my eyes to leave it alone.

"I'll call you later. I'm sorry about…" I whispered.

Antonio cut me off, "Don't apologize for me, baby. If he wants to live, then I suggest he forgets about you."

Antonio held out his hand for me to take. I closed my eyes tightly as a tear fell. I walked away from Antonio in anger.

# CHAPTER SEVENTEEN

## ANTONIO & SABRINA

$\mathcal{A}$ntonio

"Follow her and make sure she gets into my car," Antonio demanded.

Derrick starts to stand up from his chair as Antonio placed his hand on his shoulder.

"I wouldn't do that if I were you, Derrick Smith. Address, 3498 Howard Rd.; mother, Claire and father, Derrick Sr., living at Chester Peak. My reach is far and wide. If you even think of approaching, looking, or saying Sabrina's name, I will pay a visit to your little family, Mr. Smith."

Derrick had a look of fear, and utter disbelief. I picked up a piece of chicken off Sabrina's plate, popped it into my mouth, and smiled as I walked out of the restaurant.

Sabrina was pissed off at me for crashing her date. I walked outside and entered the limo. Sabrina tried to slide all the way over toward the door to avoid my touch. "You know I can't let you go," I informed her.

"I'm not doing this with you. After tonight, stay away from me!" Sabrina yelled.

"Fuck that!" I shouted.

"We aren't together. I don't belong to you!" Sabrina screamed.

I waved her off with my hand and told the driver to head to her place.

"How did you know I was here?" Sabrina asked.

"I've had you followed for the last few weeks," I stated nonchalantly and shrugged my shoulder like it was no big deal.

"Are you serious?" Sabrina replied.

"Sabrina, you need to understand, you have my heart. When you left, I just couldn't take it. I tried to stay away. Carlo suggested giving you a little space. I couldn't last a week. I called you, tried to even get into your building, but you refused my visits. You left me with no choice," I said and shrugged.

The car pulled up to her apartment building.

"I suggest you forget about me, or I'll have no choice but to call the police on you," Sabrina suggested.

I laughed in her face, and she stormed out of the car and walked up to her apartment door.

I followed her. She fumbled to get her key out of her purse.

"Baby, you can run, but I'll always have eyes on you. After our first meeting in Ryde, when we made eye contact, you had me. I refuse to let you go," I explained.

"We are done. Do you hear me?" Sabrina said vehemently.

Sabrina smacked me across the face.

The smile I wore disappeared. I jacked her up against the wall.

"Don't make me spank you. Keep your hands to yourself, Sabrina," I grumbled.

I could tell she felt flustered from the closeness of my

body on top of hers. I tried to move in closer for a kiss, but she tilted her head out of the way.

"I leave for a business meeting out of the country in the morning. I'll call you when I get back in town, and you better answer," I told her.

I let her go, and she started to walk inside.

"And if I don't?" Sabrina replied.

"Then I'll find you, and it won't be pretty, baby. Your ass is looking to get spanked, and you know I love it when you scream my name," I boasted about the way I had her during sex.

**Sabrina**

I was speechless as I walked inside, closing the door. I knew he'd find me, and my best bet was to stop running. My mind knew the relationship wouldn't work. My heart just didn't match my mind. With him out of the country, maybe I had a chance of getting over our issues.

**Antonio**

We had an early-morning flight the next morning, going back home to Italy for an important meeting with Camilla's father. She was trying her best to get her family to manipulate me into marrying her. All we'd ever had was sex between us; feelings were never involved on my end. She was playing a dangerous game if she thought I would agree to this fake marriage. After last night, I needed a distraction from Sabrina. She needed time to accept her place in my world. I decided to give her a few days to get over her so-called date she had.

"What the fuck did you do last night?" Carlo asked.

"What are you talking about?" I replied.

Carlo placed his cup of coffee down and looked over at me in disbelief.

"You need to leave her alone and let her be happy," Carlo suggested.

"Stay out of my love life and worry about yours," I muttered.

"I wish I could. Somehow, your girl called my girl and stayed on the phone with her all night. That prevented me from getting my dick wet. Shit, you both need therapy."

I laughed at Carlo's admission.

"I take it Janice closed down shop last night. Sorry, brother, I couldn't let her think she could date someone else. She belongs to me, and if any man touches her, they die," I said succinctly.

"What about what she wants?" Carlo asked.

"She wants me too. I'll give her some time, but in the end, we'll be together. She'll be the next Donna of the family," I answered.

"How does she feel about that?" Carlo asked.

I looked out the window at the sky as I gathered my thoughts.

"She has no choice. I need her. I can't think, eat, or breathe without her. These last few days have been pure torture without her. I can't explain the connection we have," I explained.

Carlo agreed with my admission. I knew he felt the same about Janice, whether he could admit that to himself or not.

"Just give her some space. We need your head in the game. This deal will set us up for major moves over the Eastern Europe Cartel," Carlo said.

"I hear you. Did Camilla confirm with you after our little meeting?" I asked.

"She said Bruno is up to something. I placed a detail on her; we can't go accusing him of anything without concrete proof," Carlo said. I opened my laptop. Seeing Sabrina's face as my screensaver, I briefly wandered off in thought about my last conversation with her. I was determined to get her back.

The flight landed, and Carlo and I headed to the chauffeured car. As we entered, a woman was sitting inside, wearing shades.

"I'm glad you both could join me," Adrian Ricci said.

"Does your husband know you're here?

"Unlike your mother, my husband and I make decisions together. One of those decisions is you marrying Camilla."

Placing my shades on, I just smiled blandly at Mrs. Ricci as we drove off to our destination.

# CHAPTER EIGHTEEN

## SABRINA

**O**ne week later

After dealing with Antonio crashing my date, ignoring his calls, and never hearing back from Derrick, I talked it out with my parents. I realized that holding onto the pain from the whole situation with Alex wouldn't help with having a healthy and happy relationship.

I got off the phone with Janice and Liz determined to get my man back. I walked inside Ryde, knowing that he could probably have another girl with him. I didn't care. The bitch would have to leave. Antonio belonged to me.

Wearing a long trench coat and black pumps, the bartender looked at me suspiciously.

"Hi, is Antonio here tonight?" I asked.

"He's in the back, who's asking?"

I leaned over the counter and whispered in his ear. The bartender grinned and pointed in the direction of his office. To show my thanks, I left a tip in the jar. As I double checked my makeup and gathered my thoughts, I slowly knocked on his door.

"Come in," Antonio grumbled.

I slowly walked inside.

"I didn't think you'd take my calls, so I decided to come in person to apologize," I said.

"How's your boyfriend doing?" Antonio questioned.

"We both said some things that day, and I apologize for my part," I answered.

"Is he outside waiting on you? Great, you've apologized. You can go now," he commanded in annoyance.

Slowly taking a few deep breaths to control my anger, I furrowed my eyes at him from the disrespect.

"I guess this was a mistake," I suggested.

I began to turn around to leave. "Go ahead, do what it is you do best… run. But do me a favor this time, stay gone," Antonio stated.

I swirled around and walked back toward him.

"Fuck you, Antonio. I don't need this controlling, macho bullshit from you, too."

"Ah, so Derrick can't make you stay either? I'm surprised," Antonio replied.

I walked up to him and slapped him across the face. I could see him narrowing his eyes down on my lips, and I stared intently at him.

"I'm sorry for hitting you. I didn't mean it," I muttered.

"Just go back to your fancy life and fancy boyfriend and leave us lowlife men alone," Antonio said.

"First off, Derrick's not my boyfriend. Secondly, I have no problem with you running a nightclub. So, you can cut that bullshit right now." I paced in front of his desk.

"I want it all, do you understand me? The love, the anger, vulnerability, the lust. I want to know your thoughts and frustrations, how your day went. It's an all or nothing deal with me, and I don't share," he demanded.

"How do I know this is real and not some way for you to get your kicks?" I asked.

He walked closer to me and grabbed my hand. He pulled me toward him and gently caressed my cheek. I wrapped my arms around his waist and licked my lips. He smiled and kissed my soft lips, opening me with his tongue, dancing for dominance.

"The night we slept together scared me because you said something I never thought about," I stated.

"What did I say?" he questioned.

"Stay with me, and never leave me."

"So, I scared you away because I wanted more from the moment I saw you?" he summarized.

"Yes. Usually, I'm the one chasing the guy to keep him around." He pulled me tighter into his arms.

"What changed your mind?" he asked.

"Let's just say I had a long conversation with a friend who reminded me never to have regrets. What about you?" I asked.

"I won't apologize for what I said in your office. You pissed me off and constantly seeing that Spencer prick around you makes my skin crawl. I don't share either, Sabrina, so listen to me very carefully. Make no mistake about it, I'm not a boy. I'm a man, and you'll have to deal with me and not shut me out or run whenever something gets too heavy."

"I wasn't running from you. I was trying…" I answered.

He gave me a slow, lingering kiss, effectively stopping any further argument.

"Shut up, Sabrina. I think you have me mistaken for some guy you've dated in the past. I want your heart, soul, mind, and body. This won't be easy being in my world, but it's worth what we have between us."

He closed the space between us and slowly caressed my cheek with the back of his palm. I closed my eyes, and he laid a trail of kisses on my left and right cheek and then my lips.

"I can't guarantee you that we won't fight, and I can't say I won't barge into your office again. This is me, take it or leave it, but I'm fucking crazy over you. I can't sleep, eat, or think when you're not near me, and when you are, all I want to do is stay inside you and keep everyone else out."

I joked, "Mr. De Luca, you're such a romantic."

We both laughed.

"I know I'm not the business type of guy you're used to dating, but I promise I'll make it worth your while."

"Don't make promises you can't keep."

"Is that a challenge?"

I pulled him onto the couch and then walked over and locked the door to his office.

"Baby, what are you up to?" Antonio asked curiously.

"Seeing as how it's been a week since we've seen each other, I think we're both overdue for a little making up. Let me smell your dick," I joked.

I grinned and took off my jacket. I slowly untied my belt and let the trench coat fall on the floor, wearing nothing but black high heels and lingerie.

His eyes popped open in frustration and anger. "Did you come dressed in just that?"

"I did. So what? Nobody saw me. Let's not start another fight just yet until we made up for the first one," I answered.

I lowered myself onto his lap until I was straddling him.

"What am I going to do with you?" Antonio suggested.

"I can think of a few things, but since we only have a few minutes until the club gets going, let's just stick to having a quickie," I replied.

"Baby, with you dressed like that, I can't be quick about anything," he answered.

I slowly trailed kisses onto his neck and then placed delicate, tender kisses upon his lips. I slowly pushed my tongue in and out of his mouth before I tried to gain dominance. I stood up from his lap and lowered down to the floor while keeping eye contact and leaning up to meet him halfway into a kiss. I unbuckled his pants, and his eyes sparkled with an expression of delight that I was the cause of his hard erection. Finally, I lowered my mouth onto his cock in a slow, teasing motion while keeping eye contact.

He grabbed a fistful of my hair as I continued sucking and licking, working him to the edge of his orgasm, at the same time squeezing his balls while he made feral moans and gasps. He thrusted his hips, fucking my mouth with his dick moving back and forth inside. I could feel him hit the back of my throat with each stroke, and he pulled nearly all the way out before pushing back in again. I stroked his cock up and down.

Antonio's head fell back on the couch.

"Oh shit, that feels good, baby," he moaned.

Between the heavy breathing and strangled growls, I moved back up onto his lap and grabbed his face for a kiss while positioning his dick at my entrance. I slowly moved down to take his entire length. We both moaned in pleasure.

"Fuck, you're so big," I whispered.

"Hush… Baby, you can take it," Antonio moaned.

I rocked back and forth in slow strokes to savor the moment of our reunion.

"Bella, I missed you so fucking much. Don't ever do that shit again," Antonio groaned.

Antonio moved his hands around to grab my ass to increase the thrusts. He then grabbed my face and placed our foreheads together.

"Sabrina, will you be my girlfriend?"

I stopped moving and fell over onto his chest in laughter, and Antonio smacked me on the ass.

"Ouch, that hurt, baby," I replied.

"You love it, don't lie, and answer my question," Antonio grunted.

I moved up and down in faster thrusts as he nibbled and licked in small circles at each breasts. Sweat dripped from his brow onto my chest, and he squeezed my breasts even tighter while licking. I made a loud gasping sound. Antonio tried covering my mouth to conceal the passionate growls and moans, but I bit his hand.

"Fuck, baby, we have to stop… I need to… get back to work," Antonio growled.

A knock at the door interrupted us.

"Boss, we have some visitors out front," a guy yelled from outside the office.

"Shhh… tell them to wait," he shouted.

I started to get off him.

"What are you doing? Get back here," he demanded.

"We have plenty of time, Antonio. Besides, I have work to catch up on." I kissed Antonio on the lips as we both got dressed to leave.

"Look at me, Sabrina. This isn't over. I'll have Salvatore drive you home, and I'll meet you later."

"Don't be silly. I can drive myself," I told him.

Antonio smacked me on the ass.

"Stop trying to boss me around and do as I say," he replied.

"I'm not one of your employees or other ex-girlfriends. I'm my own person, Antonio. You should know that by now. Don't try to order me around."

"I'm trying to be a good boyfriend. The reason I like you is that you challenge me with that smartass mouth of yours, which, by the way, I need to finish fucking before the night is over with. But I want you to come home with me tonight, so we can finish talking."

I grabbed Antonio by the face and planted a kiss on his lips.

"Make sure not to forget it, either. Fine, I'll allow Salvatore to take me to my place to pick up some clothes, and I'll sleep over tonight," I answered. "Will you wake me up for breakfast in the morning?" I asked as I smiled seductively and walked away, putting a little more sway into my stride than normal.

# CHAPTER NINETEEN

## ANTONIO

$\mathcal{I}$ watched as Sabrina got into the back of my car, and Salvatore drove off.

"I see you and Sabrina made up," Carlo teased.

"Fuck you!" I growled.

"Looks like someone had a good afternoon quickie."

"Sometimes I wonder why I even talk to you."

Carlo playfully grabbed me by the arm as we walked back into the club.

"Listen, I'm all about afternoon hookups, but this is a place of business. So, next time, take it somewhere else."

"Coming from the threesome king," I said. "Please, I don't give a fuck who hears me, and if someone talks, tell them to come see me if they have a problem with it." Later that night, I pulled up to my home. I walked into my living room, looking for Sabrina. Not finding her in the kitchen or bedroom, I called her cell. Getting no answer, I grew angry until I saw the patio door open. I walked out and saw her clothes strewn on a patio chair. I quickly adjusted myself as I looked at Sabrina. As I approached, she walked out of the pool with her towel on, and I picked her up. We both gasped from the moisture on her body, and my heat pressed up against her.

"You are mine? Answer me," I demanded.

"All yours, mi amore," Sabrina said.

"God, you're beautiful," I stated, sliding my hands up and down her back.

"Baby, sssshhh," she groaned.

"Are you ready for me, baby? I need you so much, Bella," I whispered in her ear.

"Shit… Antonio…" she gasped.

Watching as her beautiful face came down from her climax, I kissed all over her face. Placing soft, gentle kisses on her forehead, right and left cheek, nose, and lips. We trembled from the high.

After a few minutes, she calmed down. I got off her and walked to the bathroom. I grabbed a towel and wiped her off. She moaned from the warm towel against her hot skin. I placed the towel on my nightstand and wrapped her in my arms against my chest, and we lay together in my bed.

# CHAPTER TWENTY

## SABRINA & ANTONIO

$\mathcal{A}$ntonio
A few days later, we sat in the back of my Porsche as we headed to my family's home for dinner. I kissed Sabrina on the nose to calm her nerves for the first visit.

"I'm nervous about this. Maybe we should reschedule for another time," she said.

"Mi amore, don't be nervous. Everyone will love you, and if they don't, who cares? I'm the one who gets to have you all to myself," I said.

"I hope you feel that way when you have to meet my family," she replied.

"You belong to me now; this pussy is mine. Do you understand me?" I answered.

We walked into my family's home. I grew up here, and I was still amazed at how beautiful it had stayed over the years. My mother installed Italian marble floors and white gauzy imported curtains from Italy hung from the floor-to-ceiling windows. The living room had a fireplace that sat with a mantel imported with black chrome sides facing forward with the large letter C in white gold, displaying the cartel logo. The dining room was an open space sitting area. We entered loudly, talking and laughing.

As we walked through the living room, every gaze fell on us, and everyone stopped talking.

My mother walked over and kissed me on the cheek and gave me a hug. Then I introduced Sabrina.

"Mother, this is Sabrina. Baby, this is my mother, Maria De Luca."

"Hi, Mrs. De Luca," she said.

"Ah, Antonio, you didn't tell me how beautiful she was. It's nice to meet you, Sabrina, and please, call me Maria."

Sabrina shot me a look as if she were a deer in headlights and squeezed my hand.

"Of course, Maria. You have a lovely home. Thank you for inviting me." Sabrina replied.

I looked over at my father, who still sat and stared at Sabrina, not giving off an impression. Everyone waited for him to make a move before anyone else got up.

He nonchalantly got up and walked out to his office.

I was fuming at his behavior, but I knew now was not the time to get into an argument with my father.

My mom felt the tension, so she graciously informed everyone that dinner was ready and to please follow her to the dining room. She guided her arm into Sabrina's and escorted her while I headed to my father's office. Sabrina glanced back at me with a scared expression, and I kissed her on the forehead before leaving.

I barged into my father's office, asking, "What was with that little show outside, Father?" I questioned.

"I will not accept this woman into our home. She may be good for a quick fuck, but you have responsibilities, son, and tradition to uphold. Don't forget that," Dad informed me.

### Sabrina

We all heard the yelling coming from Mr. De Luca's office, and Maria tried to distract everyone with conversation.

"So, Sabrina, what do you do for a living?" Maria asked.

I shifted in my seat, uncomfortable from all the attention. Antonio and his father walked into the dining room as I started to speak.

"I am a vice president at an investment firm my father created."

Antonio returned and kissed me on the cheek as he sat next to me.

Jimmy, who had also returned to the table, looked over at his wife in anger, and she stared back at him, but he ignored it and joined the conversation.

"Sabrina, I understand you've been dating my son for a few weeks, but you understand this will never go anywhere. I would hate for you to get hurt," Jimmy told me bluntly as he took a sip from his wine glass.

Everyone grew silent and looked up from eating to stare at Jimmy. Antonio glared at his father and slammed his hand down on the table. He yelled in Italian, so I couldn't understand the conversation. I swallowed the pasta down with wine, complimented his mother on the food.

"Don't ever speak to her in that manner. She is the woman I love!" Antonio shouted.

Jimmy yelled back at Antonio as Maria told everyone to leave the room.

I stood and started to walk out, but I stopped at the door and turned around.

"Mr. De Luca, I understand you have traditions. Believe me, I tried hard to stay away from Antonio, but we both know he's stubborn, and I see where he gets it from. So, you can yell and insult me all day long, but it doesn't change anything other than getting your blood pressure up. I suggest you get over it because you'll be seeing a lot of me at family dinners to come. Good night, Maria. It was a lovely meal. Antonio, I'll be in the car," I said as I strode out of the room with my head held high. Sabrina Washington cowered under no man.

**Antonio**

We entered her apartment, and she pushed me against the wall. She kissed me hard on the lips, biting my bottom lip, and roamed her hands up and down my chest. I started to move my hands up and down her shoulders, and she slapped them away. Sabrina turned around for me to unzip her dress, and it fell to the floor. I picked her up and placed her against the wall and thrust inside her before she could protest.

"Dammnit… you're so tight," I groaned.

My mouth clamped onto her nipple as she held onto me. With each thrust of my cock, I went deeper and harder until a light sheen of sweat coated my forehead and dampened my hair. Her eyes rolled to the back of her head.

Sabrina came again, digging her nails into my back. All she knew was that she needed to hold on and never let go. I moaned out and came inside her. I kept the side of my face pressed against her chest and my arms wrapped around her waist. I didn't even bother to pull out of her. We were both silent. The only sound in the room was the echo of heavy breathing. Sabrina bit and licked my neck and shoulder while squeezing my ass.

**Sabrina**

I could hear every little grunt and hot breath against my skin with each surge forward.

"Miss Washington, are you trying to take advantage of me?" Antonio groaned. "Look at me," he said.

Slowly easing his cock in and out of my opening, my thighs spread for him, and he sank between my long, shapely legs. He slid into me, holding my legs far apart as he burrowed deeper and deeper. He didn't even pause in his slow, easy thrusts. The palm of his hand massaged my clit. I sought his mouth with mine, kissing him deeply.

His strokes increased in tempo.

"Ughh, Sabrina," he moaned into my ear.

"Ohh, Antonio, wait," I moaned out.

His thrusts grew faster now.

"Fuck, you feel too good, baby. I can't control myself," Antonio said.

I grabbed his hair. My fingers dug into his scalp as my excitement built. He tore his mouth away from mine.

"Come for me!" I shouted.

"What the fuck? Shit!" he grunted aloud as his body tensed up from his orgasm.

I felt him shudder violently inside me, and I regretted that I couldn't see his face. Antonio grasped my hips and held me still, grinding deeply until his spasms calmed. He pulled out and collapsed on the floor while holding me, eyes closed, breathing hard.

"That was fantastic," I told him.

"Tell me that you're mine," he said.

I leaned up and kissed Antonio on the lips.

"I'm yours, baby," I said.

# CHAPTER TWENTY-ONE

## ANTONIO

*I* left Sabrina at her place after the big blowout at my parents' house. I headed to a meeting to get information on the rat in my father's business. I sat in my limo, contemplating if I should check on her. We didn't leave with the best experience from my father's racist view toward Sabrina. He knew deep down that we loved each other, but the cartel required pure Sicilian blood in the family.

I looked down at my watch. Noticing the time, my bodyguard looked over at me through the rearview mirror and nodded the signal to get ready. I nodded back in agreement. It was time to finalize and end the Russian trade deal my father had started fifteen years ago with our cartel. It had brought nothing but trouble for the family from the feds and local police. Even though he had the police in his pocket, I needed to get things cleaned up and not be distracted by outside people, including Sabrina.

The door opened, and I stepped out. I smoothed out my long black jacket, tie, and gun. Carlo pulled up next to me just as I was about to walk into the meeting.

Carlo jumped out of the car with three more body-guards. One stood at least six foot six, and the other one was about my height with a little more muscles in the arms. He had glacial-blue eyes. One had a shaved head, and the other wore his hair pulled back in a sleek ponytail. They each wore tracksuits and were holding AK47s on the side, with black glasses over their eyes, scoping out the surrounding area.

I approached Carlo.

"Are we ready?" I asked.

"We have three on the roof, two in the back, and two standing up front, guarding the door," Carlo replied.

I smirked in amusement.

"These idiots have no idea what's about to happen, thinking they can come to my city and take over my territories, run deals behind my back," I replied, sarcastically.

Carlo motioned for two of the bodyguards to walk in front and the other in the back.

"Let's get this over with. I have a date in an hour," Carlo stated.

"Stop thinking about pussy, you pussy…" I chuckled.

As the doors opened, a quiet calm overcame the room as I walked inside. Sensing the Don of De Luca Cartel entering, each gentleman stood out of respect to acknowl-edge me.

"Have a seat, gentleman," I announced.

Looking each man in the eye, I wanted to see if anything looked suspicious.

"I hear we have a problem," Vlad, the Russian Capo said.

"We do actually, and I'm here to solve it," I replied.

I walked over to the table and sat at the head. I pulled out my gun and sat it on the table, knowing it wouldn't intimidate these men. It needed to distract them from what was about to go down tonight. Clearing my throat and taking off my jacket slowly, I pulled out a cigar.

"Would anyone like one? It's the best in the city, straight from Italy," I suggested.

Everyone looked at each other, then at me, and said no.

"Your loss. I called this meeting because it's become apparent that you can't seem to listen when I tell you this is my city," I stated bluntly.

Another Russian gentleman started to speak, but I cut him off.

"I didn't ask for an answer," I demanded.

Carlo walked around the table as I continued talking.

"You see, my father isn't running the De Luca Cartel anymore. I am, and as you know, my first business responsibility is ending all gun deals with you," I informed.

Vlad didn't like the way the conversation was going. He slowly reached for his gun. At the same time, he made eye contact with one of my bodyguards. Unbeknownst to Carlo and myself, some of the bodyguards were apparently working against the cartel.

Vlad made the signal of blinking his eyes twice and started to speak as a distraction so they could get a shot off on either one of us.

All of a sudden, we heard TATT...TATTTT...

BOOM!

Someone tossed the table over, and Carlo tried to get a shot off, then jump for cover. I was too slow and only got a head shot off on one of them.

"Tony, get down!" Carlo screamed.

"Carlo... Carlo... Fuckkk!" I yelled.

Shots came from every angle. Vlad rushed and shot one of the bodyguards with me. I noticed and shot Vlad in the chest three times. Without looking at him, a tall figure walked up and shot me in the left arm and back.

"Shit… Carlo," I groaned out slowly.

Carlo looked up right as I fell to my knees. Not paying attention to his own safety, he shot at any and everything as the other bodyguards from outside closed in on the Russian mob.

He made it over to me just as blood spilled out of my mouth.

"Tony, listen to me," Carlo stated.

Carlo held my head up and took his jacket off to keep me warm. He quickly grabbed the phone from his pocket and called for backup.

"Bruno. Listen, goddammit. We need backup and shelter," Carlo bellowed.

"What happened?" Bruno asked.

"Tony was hit," Carlo said, somberly.

"Where the fuck is my brother?" Bruno shouted angrily.

"I have him, just get here. It was a setup," Carlo yelled.

Carlo hung up on Bruno, screaming through the phone.

"Think about Sabrina. You can't leave her," Carlo said.

"Tell her… I love…" I muttered softly.

Slowly, darkness took my vision as my eyes rolled into the back of my head, and I passed out.

# CHAPTER TWENTY-TWO

## CARLO

"*A*ntonio, wake up, man. Please don't do this," Carlo yelled, pressing on the bullet wound to stop the bleeding.

Bruno and his team busted inside with Jimmy De Luca right behind him.

They ran toward Antonio and me. I motioned for him to check Antonio's vitals and help to pick him up.

"How is my son?" Jimmy asked.

"I need to get him to a hospital, Don, right now. Time is critical," Dr. Benjamin said.

"He better not die. If I lose my son, you lose yours. Do I make myself clear?" Jimmy demanded.

Dr. Benjamin agreed with his statement and walked off with the bodyguards behind him, carrying Antonio outside to the car, then heading toward the hospital.

"Carlo, meet me at the hospital. I need to contact my wife about this. Bruno, find out who did this and bring them to me," Jimmy commanded.

Bruno took out his gun and checked the chamber. He walked over to the dead bodies of three Russians. Looking into each of their eyes, he shot each one and looked back at Jimmy and me.

"I'll have a name by the time you make it to the hospital," Bruno said confidently.

Thirty minutes later, Maria, Jimmy, and I sat in the hospital, waiting to hear an update about Antonio's condition.

"Why did you send him out blind?" Maria asked.

"My love, now is not the time," Jimmy sighed with frustration.

Maria stood with bloated and flushed eyes, with dark circles around them from crying, and smacked Jimmy across the face.

"Don't you dare tell me it's not the right time. That's my son in that room, fighting for his life!" Maria screamed.

"Maria, calm down. Please, Bella," Jimmy grumbled.

Maria paced the floor, shaking her head in anger.

Bruno walked into the hospital just as the doctor walked out to give an update on Antonio's condition.

"How is he? Please tell me he's going to be all right?" Maria asked with a shaky voice.

"Maria, please sit," Dr. Benjamin asked.

Maria backs up from the doctor as tears fell unchecked from her eyes.

"My baby! Oh God, no!" Maria shouts.

Jimmy grabbed Maria and hugged her as Dr. Benjamin tried to explain.

"Antonio's a fighter. He's alive. He did have a close call, but we got him stabilized," Dr. Benjamin said.

"Thank you, Jesus," I shouted.

Maria pulled away from Jimmy.

"He's okay? Really? When can we see him?" Maria asked.

"Yes, he's alive, but unfortunately, he fell into a coma while we had him open on the table," Dr. Benjamin replied.

"What?" Maria said, surprised.

Dr. Benjamin escorted the family back to Antonio's room.

"Follow me, and I'll show you his room. We have him sedated so his body can heal itself," Dr. Benjamin informed us.

"How long are you keeping him like this?" Jimmy inquired.

"At the moment, three to four weeks. Maybe longer. It's all up to Antonio at this point," Dr. Benjamin replied.

"Is he in pain? My poor baby," Maria inquired.

"No, he can still hear us. He's just in a deep sleep. I'll let you decide who wants to stay tonight. But we can't have any more visitors tonight," Dr. Benjamin suggested.

Jimmy and Maria both agreed that she would stay as Bruno and I walked out.

"Who did this?" I asked.

"You wouldn't believe it if I told you." Bruno pulled out a cigarette and lit it while we waited on Jimmy.

"I thought it was you at first. Seeing the way you reacted when I called," I told him.

"My brother's a spoiled brat. But I love him, and I'd do anything to protect the family," Bruno replied.

Bruno took another pull from the cigarette.

Jimmy walked out toward his limo.

"Meet me at the house. We need to finish this. I can't have your mother hating me," Jimmy mumbled.

"She doesn't hate you, Pop. Give her time," Bruno replied.

Jimmy waved off Bruno's statement.

"Who's guarding Antonio's room?" I inquired.

"Salvatore. So, who exactly pulled this bullshit?" Jimmy asked.

"Too many people. I have to confirm another name. Let's meet at the house in an hour," Bruno suggested.

"Tell me now," Jimmy shouted.

"Pop, listen," Bruno said somberly.

Jimmy walked up close to Bruno and grabbed him aggressively, jacking him up by the collar and pushing him up against the car.

"Give me a name," Jimmy demanded, angrily.

Bruno looked over at me and then at Jimmy.

"Alfredo," Bruno said.

# CHAPTER TWENTY-THREE

## ANTONIO

*Month Later*

I walked inside and noticed Elliott, one of our closest workers and a family friend, strapped down to a table with his hands covered and feet nailed down. His mouth was duct taped. A small silence came across the room as they waited for me to begin. Normally, it would be Bruno handling all interrogations and torture, but he was handling other family business. Everyone knew Bruno was the muscle of the family, and I was the brain. I had way more sadistic, unorthodox ways and lethal power than Bruno would ever have, which was why my father chose me to take over the family.

I grabbed the gun from one of his men and slowly walked around the man sitting, without saying a word. Gliding in a predatory manner, I just waited and stalked, letting the anticipation boil to a simmer. I snatched the duct tape off his swollen lips.

"Arghhh!" Elliott screamed out in pain.

I leaned up close, right in front of his face. "Do you have anything to say for yourself? Before you start, this is a one-time gesture of faith. If I don't like what you say, a bullet goes into one part of your body every time you answer wrong. They'll have you buried looking like Swiss cheese. Your family won't even be able to recognize you."

"Please, Tony, you know me," Elliott pleaded.

I grabbed a chair and sat down to speak with Elliott.

"Leave the room," I demanded.

"Tony, just end it, and let's move on," Carlo replied.

The bodyguards looked at Carlo and me, wondering if he could calm me down. Dad and his man on the inside, Detective Blake, a local police officer, walked into the warehouse as I continued asking Elliott about the shooting.

"Please, Jimmy, tell him. I had nothing to do with the shooting," Elliott whined.

I stood and shot Elliott in his left kneecap.

"Fuckk…. Shit… please stop!" Elliott screamed in anguish with tears streaming down his face.

The man nodded and spoke, but he was hoarse from all the screaming. I splashed his face with cold water to keep him coherent.

"Sonny Bishop hired me to get information. He works for Alfredo; that's all I know."

I looked him directly in the eye before standing back up.

"Mr. Elliott, one thing we don't tolerate is betrayal. You've worked with my family for many years. It'll be tough to get someone else to replace you, but it can't be helped. I promise your family will grieve, and I'll think about giving you a proper burial."

I pointed the gun right at his temple and pulled the trigger. I then handed the gun to our bodyguard and walked out.

"Burn his body and find me Alfredo, now!" I shouted.

I walked out of the warehouse, and Jimmy grabbed me by the arm.

"Tony, let me handle him," Dad stated.

I looked down at his arm, and my father let me go. I squared my shoulders, walking closer to my father with a mean look on my face.

"You don't run the show anymore. Remember, Pop? I'm the Don now, and this son of a bitch tried to kill me. You think I'll let this slide?" I yelled.

Bruno and Carlo followed me as I walked off from our father, looking sad at the thought of his son killing his only brother.

# CHAPTER TWENTY-FOUR

## SABRINA

Leaving for work, I saw Sal parked out front.

"Sal, what are you doing here?" I asked.

Sal started the car up and gestured for me to get inside. I knew that Antonio was overprotective, especially since the dinner with his parents a month or so ago. After his shooting, he became increasingly overprotective with bodyguards everywhere. Checking in at all hours of the day and night. Carlo called me from the hospital, and I had Janice drive because I was so frightened to get behind the wheel with all the thoughts swirling on if he was dead or alive. That time made me think of what I could have missed out on for my future.

I entered my office twenty minutes later. Janice walked toward me as I placed my coat and purse underneath my desk.

"Long time no see, stranger," Janice said.

I felt embarrassed that I hadn't seen my friends or family much since I'd been with Antonio and sighed as I sat at my desk.

"I'm sorry. It's been an exhausting few weeks. How

about we do lunch and call Liz so we can all catch up?" I suggested.

"Okay. In the meantime, can you look over this new account I have?" she asked.

"Sure, how are things with Carlo going?"

Janice had a small smirk on her face.

"I can't describe it, but I think I'm in love," Janice said.

I looked at my friend with amusement. "Really? That's new. He must be something special."

"He is, and I want to introduce him to my parents."

"I think that's a great idea. But do you understand what he does for a living?" Overall, the many nights I tossed and turned with worry about Antonio, I wasn't stupid. I knew he had a hand in something illegal. Being the underboss wasn't the first thing that came to my mind. Taking the time to embrace my new life with a mobster was different from what I grew up with. If I wanted him in my life, then I needed to make sacrifices. After all, he just recovered from a gunshot wound.

Janice looked at me with an all-knowing look.

"I understand. I can't let him go. In a short amount of time, I've grown to love and need him. When I'm away from him, I grow restless. I can't explain it."

I nodded in agreement.

"How about we talk about this later over some cocktails?"

Janice got up and hugged me, then walked out of my office.

# CHAPTER TWENTY-FIVE

## ANTONIO

I walked into my father's office building. Bruno, Carlo, Dad, and the other underbosses and his bodyguard sat in the basement with Detective Blake.

"What's all this?" I asked.

Bruno pulled out a seat and motioned for me to sit.

"I've asked you all to be here because we have a delicate situation on our hands." As my father spoke, he stared at me.

I knew my father was talking about Sabrina, but I refused to get into another blowup over it.

"I've had your little girlfriend researched, and we need to discuss the best way to handle this." I glared in anger as my father continued talking. "I understand this is an infatuation, but she can't be a part of this family. Do you know who her father is, Antonio?"

"Yes, I know of her father, and it doesn't change anything," I said.

My father told everyone else in the room, and they all looked startled and frowned.

"Sabrina's father is Jonathan Washington of Washington Finance, a very high-profile person, which is something this family can't be around. I warned you to end this, but now you've created a bigger issue for this family."

I tapped my finger on the desk as my father continued to speak. Carlo looked at me in disbelief that my father wanted to kill his son's girlfriend. To everyone's shocked expression, Bruno interrupted his father's impassioned speech. "Don, I've met this Sabrina Washington. She's a very cool girl, and under any other terms, I would be the first to say we should make this problem disappear, but as you say, her father is a very high-profile individual. If anything happens, we'll have a lot of people knocking on our door," Bruno said. Bruno turned his head and looked me in the eyes. "I suggest Antonio breaks up with her and strongly suggests that she stay away from him. If he can't persuade her, then I'll be more than happy to make this problem go away."

I started to get up and yell at my brother.

"I will disregard that last part of your statement, seeing as how we're related, but I promise, if anything happens to her or a piece of hair is out of place, I will come at you so hard that I'll forget you're my brother."

"Antonio, silence. Detective Blake here suggested we hold off on your little bambina disappearing as well, so you have him to thank, but this timetable of a breakup needs to happen today. Otherwise, my gratitude won't last for very long."

I looked over at Detective Blake and my father. I walked out and headed to my car while texting Sabrina. I was trying to figure out a plan to hold off my father and brother from hurting her.

*Antonio: Where are you?*

*Sabrina:* I'm having lunch with Janice and Liz.
*Antonio:* I need to see you later tonight.
*Sabrina:* Is everything ok?
*Antonio:* Just be home later. We need to talk.

# CHAPTER TWENTY-SIX

## SABRINA

*Two hours later.*

"So, what's been happening, lady?" Liz said. Janice and I both looked at each other and laughed. Liz had a perplexed expression on her face.

"Well, I've been working on trying to close a big deal and still dating Carlo. I have no complaints. He's the best, and I'm in love." I sat at lunch with Janice and Liz, catching up from the last few weeks.

Liz looked at Janice with a shocked expression. We all knew that Janice couldn't be tamed or tied down to just one man, so this was entirely new.

"Really, you and Carlo from the nightclub? How long has this been going on?" Liz asked.

"Since the first night. I guess we just clicked, and I'm…"

Before she could continue, my phone vibrated, interrupting them. I looked down at the text message from Antonio. Something was wrong. I had been feeling nervous and agitated. So, I turned my phone off and continued drinking and listening to Janice and Liz.

"So, Sabrina, how is everything with you?"

"Actually, guys, I'm not feeling so well. I think I'll take a rain check on lunch. Next time on me, okay?" I got up, kissed them both on the cheek, and headed out. They looked at me and then at each other as I walked out.

I headed back to the office to finish up work as Spencer caught me in the conference room. "Hey, you seem to be somewhere else. Is that paperwork that interesting?" Spencer questioned.

I placed the paperwork down. "Hi, Spencer. What's up?" I replied.

"I was looking to see if you had any plans for Friday night. I wanted to talk about some business over dinner," he asked.

I knew Antonio would go crazy if I were ever seen in public with another man on a date, especially with Spencer.

"I'll have to pass on dinner, but we can talk business right now. What's up?"

"Actually, it has to be Friday. It's a huge deal, and I don't want to lay my cards on the table without us having confirmation." Spencer pushed.

I furrowed my eyebrows at Spencer, knowing he may have ulterior motives for this dinner. "Listen, how about we discuss this another day? I need to be getting home," I told him.

Thirty minutes later, I walked into my apartment, placing my keys on the table. I decided to lie down for a few minutes to gather my thoughts. Knowing Antonio was picking me up for dinner, I gathered up the strength to jump in the shower. A few minutes after taking a shower, I walked into the kitchen to grab something to eat. Turning the TV on and watching a rerun of Insecure, I contemplated how my relationship was something like a TV show. My entire engagement to Alex was rocky, and he ended up cheating. Then I started up another relationship or situationship. He was ten times more the man Alex was. My heart wouldn't allow it to cut him off.

*"He's mine."* I smiled to myself.

# CHAPTER TWENTY-SEVEN

## ANTONIO & SABRINA

**A**ntonio
I headed to Sabrina's apartment to end things before it got too complicated., and thirty-five minutes later, I knocked on her door.

"Hey, babe." She answered the door and kissed me on the lips.

"Sabrina, we need to talk," I said.

"What's wrong? Talk to me, Antonio," she asked.

"I can't do this anymore. We have to stop seeing each other," I told her.

"Baby, you're not making any sense. Sit down, let's talk about this."

"I know what I said about us being together, but I've changed my mind," I said in frustration.

Sabrina walked into the kitchen to get a bottle of wine and a glass of scotch for me.

"I'm not accepting this, Antonio. We both wanted this, and you forced me to make a decision about being with you. Now, after everything we've been through, you want to break up? Are you seeing someone else? Is it that Camilla girl?" she questioned.

"I'm not seeing anyone else. It's just a busy time for me, that's all. I'm sorry this happened, but we can't be together. It's better if we stay away from each other. We both knew from the start that this could never be anything."

"I know about your family's business, Antonio, and I'm not afraid of it, or you. Please, just stay with me, and we'll work it out," Sabrina replied.

She leaned in to kiss me, and I groaned in pleasure from her lips.

"Who told you?" I demanded.

"That doesn't matter. I don't like it, but if I want you in my life, I have to accept all of you," Sabrina answered.

"Tell me who the fuck is talking to you about me!" I yelled. She tried to push me back and walk out. I grabbed her tightly by her waist and whispered in her ear, "If it was that Spencer prick, I promise you, he'll be dead by the morning," I harshly replied.

Sabrina tensed up at my words.

"Let me go. It wasn't Spencer, you asshole. It was your brother!" Sabrina shouted.

I held back my shock from her answer. I frowned and grabbed my phone to call my brother. Before I could, Sabrina took my phone and threw it across the room.

"No, we handle this now. Leave everyone out of this. I mean you said you could handle me, right? So let me see the big bad Antonio. Ohh, no… wait… it's Don of the De Luca Cartel. Shall I curtsy or kiss the ring?" Sabrina sarcastically replied.

Sensing my anger rising, I decided to shut her up another way.

I picked her up in my arms and walked her toward the bedroom. Placing her on the bed, I admired her for a few minutes and rubbed up and down her thighs. I swiftly unbuckled my pants and tore off her panties, fighting to calm her down and show her how much she meant to me. We were both moaning and gasping from the feel of my erection near her beautiful pussy. I angrily bit Sabrina on her neck and shoulder for not rejecting me the first minute I walked into her life. She turned over and placed her hands flat on the mattress, holding tight to the bed sheets with her ass pushed up toward me.

"Spread your legs more for me."

I slowly inserted my thumb into the ring of clenched muscles, dipping it in and out.

"I own this," I growled.

I reached over and pleasured her clit.

**Sabrina**

His groans of pleasure encouraged me to suck harder and move faster. I wriggled my tongue against the underside of his cock as I sucked him deep. When he was buried deep in my throat again, I hummed and reached down to knead my breast in slow movements.

"Baby, you are so wet."

His tongue followed my fingers, and his hips convulsed. He held my thighs firmly against the bed, spread wide open for him.

"So sweet," Antonio moaned.

"Please," I begged.

We both collapsed breathless onto the bed, and he pulled me to his chest as we fell into a deep sleep.

I woke up reaching out for him, but I only found a note on my pillow:

*Bella, I'm sorry, but this is for the best. We can't continue. My father was right. This would never be anything more. It's best you find someone worthy of you- Ti Amore, Antonio.*

I fell into my pillow crying for the next few hours,

thinking about what happened last night when my phone rang.

"I can't talk right now, Janice." I sniffed into the phone.

"What's going on, Sabrina? I got a text from Carlo this morning saying that Antonio's going crazy at the club. He's just yelling at everybody."

I got out of bed and went to the bathroom to get dressed for the day while still talking to Janice.

"We broke up last night. Janice, it's over, and I don't want to talk about it," I answered.

"I'm sorry to hear that. I thought you guys had something real. Are you coming into the office today?" Janice asked.

I knew that I couldn't escape Antonio from my home or work life. I pretended as if the call was dropping so I could get ready for the workday.

"Boo, I have to go. My phone…." I muttered.

"Bitch, don't hang up on me!" Janice yelled.

Thinking about Antonio and his bullshit excuses was the last thing I wanted to deal with. He made me fall in love, and he promised never to break my heart. I felt my chest tighten at the thought of seeing him give my love to another woman. That broke my heart. He was just like Alex.

"Ughh!!!" I screamed.

I went back to lie in bed, crying again. Thinking about Antonio with someone else felt like a death to me. This was stronger than my feelings for Alex. I had no other choice but to try to move on. I tried calling Antonio's phone. The call was finally picked up, and I could hear a loud noise in the background.

"Hello?" Camilla answered, giggling.

I couldn't believe how fast he moved on.

"Hello?" Camilla asked.

Suddenly, I heard shuffling on the other end, and the phone hung up. Deciding to move on as well, I realized that I was done with Antonio De Luca. No man would ever have my heart.

**Antonio**

Later that night in Ryde, I continued yelling and berating all my employees at the club, trying to get all my frustrations out.

Camilla walked into my office. She sat on top of my desk.

"Baby, the place is on fire tonight." Camilla chuckled.

She fixed my tie as I stared into her eyes.

"What's wrong?" Camilla asked.

"Nothing," I answered.

"This is for the best; she couldn't handle our world," Camilla suggested.

"When are your parents making the announcement?" I asked.

"This weekend. I'm so excited. We're finally getting married," Camilla purred.

"Camilla Ricci, let me remind you, I'll never love you. This is all business," I replied.

She smiled and placed a kiss on my cheek.

"Whatever you say, baby. Besides, you can learn to love me again. After your shooting and helping you find the snitch, we'll grow to love each other again. Just give it time," Camilla suggested.

"I need some air," I said.

I pushed Camilla out of my lap. She watched my somber look and smiled in glee for manipulating the entire situation and getting me back in her clutches.

"Are you listening to me?" I walked up to her and saw that she was zoned out. I waved my hand in front of her face. She finally blinked after a few minutes.

"I'm sorry, what did you…"

Carlo walking inside interrupted Camilla.

"Tony, we got some information on Alfredo," Carlo told me.

Carlo looked over at Camilla to leave. She looked at me for support.

"She can stay," I suggested.

Dumbfounded, apparently Carlo was taken aback by me agreeing to let Camilla listen in on our conversation.

"Tony, you can't be serious!" Carlo bellowed.

Camilla walked over and sat in my chair as though she was running things.

"Very, so get to talking, Carlo. I'm soon to be the new Donna of this family. I know the ins and outs of this. It's best for all of us to keep me in the loop," Camilla replied.

Carlo looked down at Camilla in anger. I could tell he was shaking his head at me for bringing Camilla back around.

# CHAPTER TWENTY-EIGHT

## SABRINA

*Four weeks later*
I decided to head out for dinner with Spencer, looking to start over without Antonio. I continued to explain to Spencer that this was just a friendly dinner and nothing more. We walked into Antonio's Restaurant, unbeknownst to either of us that Antonio was having dinner with an old girlfriend.

"What are we doing here, Spencer?" I asked.

"We have reservations. I heard it's the best place in town and always booked in advance for reservations. Come on, let's go. You need a break from the craziness."

"I'm not sure about this place," I said.

We continued talking and walking further inside. As we approached the dining area, Spencer placed his arm around my waist, pulling me close to his body as though I belonged to him. I narrowed my eyes down at his hand around my waist. I moved back up to his eye line toward whatever had his attention from the tight squeeze he held me with. I came face to face with Antonio and Camilla sitting at a table together. I stopped in my tracks when

Antonio held a hard glare. We stared into each other's eyes for the longest time before anyone made a sound.

Spencer pulled me closer to him, leaving his hand on my lower back.

Antonio, with his possessive nature, clenched his fists together.

I turned to Spencer and said, "Let's go somewhere else."

"Sabrina, I'm not afraid of him. You can't let him run you off," he said.

Antonio rose from his seat and walked over to us.

"Get your hands off her," he said.

We both turned to Antonio in shock.

"Listen, Mr. De Luca, I'm not on the clock at the moment. So, that means it's after hours, and I'm on a date," Spencer replied.

Antonio turned to look at me with a mixed expression of anger, hurt, and disgust.

"Are you dating this asshole?" he asked.

"It's none of your business who I see, and for your information, he's my friend. He's been there for me since you left me. So, you don't have the right to question my social life based on what I see tonight," I announced, nodding over at his table.

"Sabrina, honey," Spencer replied.

Before he could finish his sentence, Antonio had Spencer hoisted up by his throat and called over his body-guards. Camilla and I both looked on in shock. Everyone in the restaurant started to get up to leave.

Spencer tried his best to get out of Antonio's grip as I yelled at Antonio to put him down.

"What the fuck do you think you're doing with Sabrina, huh? Answer me. I promise you one thing, the night won't end the way you thought."

Camilla tried calling Carlo to come over and help calm the situation, but he didn't pick up.

"Antonio, please leave him out of this. I swear to God if you don't let him go, I'll never forgive you," I screamed.

Antonio turned around and looked into my eyes. I stood with my arms across my chest, with my upper lip formed into a frown. I knew that I looked hurt and afraid of him for the first time. He let go of Spencer and told him to get out before he changed his mind.

I started to walk toward Spencer, but Antonio grabbed my wrist to stop me.

"I said he could go. We need to talk," Antonio demanded. I pulled my arm out of his grip.

"We have nothing to talk about. If I remember correctly, you broke up with me. Stay the fuck away from me," I snapped.

Spencer walked out with me, and Antonio motioned for his bodyguards to stop us at the door.

We both turned around. Spencer pulled his phone out of his pocket, and I stopped him.

"It's fine. Just leave, Spencer. I'll talk to you tomorrow," I told him.

"I'm not leaving you with these thugs. I'll call the police; this is harassment," Spencer stated.

"Please, just go. He won't hurt me. Just do as I say, and I promise I'll call you tomorrow," I said.

I walked toward Antonio and went with him to the bathroom. Spencer started to walk toward me, but the bodyguards quickly moved him outside as Antonio turned his head toward Camilla.

# CHAPTER TWENTY-NINE

## ANTONIO

"*I*'m sorry for the interruption. I'll call you tomorrow so we can talk."

"Antonio, let her go. It's time we worked on us and our future," Camilla stated.

I stood from my seat, annoyed with Camilla's interruption.

"I've told you it's over between us. Just have Sal take you home." I replied, annoyed with her presence.

Heading toward the bathroom, I stopped at the door, trying to gather myself before walking inside. Sabrina turned around and slapped me with an open palm.

"I hate you!" Sabrina yelled loudly.

Feeling the sting from her slap, I held in my anger and rubbed the pain away, smirking at her in amusement.

"What the fuck are you doing with that jackass Spencer?"

"Who I date is none of your business. You broke up with me, or did you forget?" Sabrina blurted sarcastically.

I moved toward Sabrina in a predatory motion, ready to devour her lips.

"Any and everything you do is my business, or did you forget whom you belonged to?" I asked.

"Antonio, I'm done with this bullshit, do you understand? Don't fucking touch me."

Sabrina knew the minute we got close, she wouldn't be able to resist me, and the love she had would surface all over again.

"I can't do this anymore!" Sabrina yelled.

"Shh… I miss you, baby. Please forgive me," I asked.

I slowly grabbed Sabrina by her waist, guided my hands up her arms, and gently stroked her cheeks. I leaned in and kissed her on the lips. She kept her eyes open in disbelief that I was kissing her after a four-week separation.

She slowly closed her eyes and parted her lips, accepting my awaiting tongue. We kissed with so much passion and anger over not being together.

Picking Sabrina up and placing her on the bathroom counter, I broke off kissing her lips. I slowly lingered, kissing her neck and cheek. Rubbing my hand up and down her thighs. Praying she would forgive me for causing her so much pain.

"I can't. Stop, please," she demanded.

I ignored her refusal between kisses.

"I said stop! You broke my heart. I can't go back!" Sabrina screamed.

She pushed me away and got off the counter. She walked out of the bathroom door, but I grabbed her by the waist, stopping her before she made it back to her date.

"Baby, I know I hurt you, and I promised I would never do that, but you have to understand it wasn't my choice," I said.

She turned around and looked me in the eye.

"What does that mean? It wasn't your choice?" Sabrina asked.

"Bella, please, I love you. Please just come with me to my place so we can talk. Afterward, if you want to go home, I'll have Sal take you. You'll never have to see me again."

Not looking in my direction, she started to walk out.

"Okay, I'll go and listen, but promise you won't hurt Spencer," she said.

I looked at her in disbelief.

"What the fuck is he to you?" I questioned.

"I could ask the same thing to you about Camilla, but I already know the answer to that question." We walked out to Salvatore waiting with the door open.

Fifteen minutes later, Salvatore pulled up to my home. I got out and tried to grab Sabrina's hand, but she smacked it away. I looked to Salvatore for help, but he just patted me on the shoulder, said to give her some time, and to be honest with her.

I opened the door for Sabrina and tried escorting her to my office, but she walked over to the living room and sat on the couch and crossed her legs.

"All right, start talking. I don't have all night," Sabrina commanded.

Placing her arms underneath her breasts, she glared at me in anger.

I made a drink as I gathered my thoughts in silence. I then turned my phone off, making sure no one disturbed me. I handed the drink to Sabrina, but she refused it.

"Since when do you not drink?" I asked.

"I'm not in the mood. Just say what you need to say so we can move on separately."

I walked over and sat next to Sabrina. I grabbed her face and placed a long, lingering kiss on her lips.

"What if I don't want to be separated from you?" I questioned. I could tell she was embarrassed from being so close to me. She attempted to get up, but I grabbed her by the waist and positioned her on my lap.

"I want you back. I need you, baby. My life has no meaning without you. Please, forgive me. I can't breathe without you."

Sabrina looked into my eyes. I could tell she was searching for honesty.

"I wish you would have done this a week or two ago. It's too late," she said.

I shook my head, refusing to let her go.

"I'll do anything, please. Just listen to your heart. You know we belong together. I didn't want to leave you, but my business was getting too close to home. I needed to get you far away from it before something happened," I admitted.

Sabrina listened intently to what I was saying.

"So, you didn't break up with me to be with Camilla?" Sabrina asked.

I kissed Sabrina's hand, arm, and shoulder, up to her neck and lips.

"Baby, you're the only woman for me, mi amore," I confessed once again.

Sabrina looked deeply into my eyes before speaking. "And what about your family and tonight with Camilla?"

I stopped kissing her and moved her off my lap.

"I can't talk to you about my business. If we're together, you'll be separate from that world. It has to be this way for your safety. I promise the only reason I went out with Camilla was that she had something to tell me. I'm not sure what, but she doesn't matter anymore. So, can we start over? I'm ready to take you to bed and make love to you. It's been so long."

I continued to kiss Sabrina all over her neck, cheeks, forehead, and lips as she tried to keep me at arm's length.

"What's wrong, Bella? Talk to me," I pleaded.

"I need to tell you something, and I'm not sure how you'll take it," Sabrina hesitated.

I was worried and angry at her hesitation. Suddenly, Bruno and Carlo busted through my door with guns drawn.

We jumped up from the intrusion.

"Why the hell didn't you answer my calls?" Bruno questioned.

"Antonio, we need to speak with you privately," Carlo said.

I nodded to them, and they came into my office.

"Baby, I need to handle some business. Can you wait for me here, or grab something to eat? I'll be back in about an hour," I said.

Sabrina looked dumbfounded at the abrupt ending of the conversation.

"Actually, I'm going to head home and when you figure out what you want, call me. Better yet, don't call me. I'm done," she demanded.

I looked at Sabrina as she walked out on me. I started to chase after her when Carlo stopped me.

"Let her go, man. We have a bigger issue at the warehouse."

I pushed Carlo's hand out of the way and watched as Sabrina left. I decided I would give her until tomorrow to think about everything, but she would be my wife, whether she liked it or not.

"Fine, tell me what's going on as we drive over," I replied gruffly.

Carlo, Bruno, and I all climbed into his car, loading up our weapons.

"I looked into the identity of the snitch and the missing

money, and everything traced back to Uncle Alfredo," Bruno said.

"Shit…!" I shouted.

"Pop knows, and he wants him brought to the house," Bruno said.

"Did we recover the guns at all?" I asked.

Carlo shook his head.

"Damnit!" I yelled.

"He had to have someone working with him," Carlo replied.

"See, people are going to make me bring the beast out," I groaned. "Call and check on Sabrina for me."

"She's fine. Didn't you have Salvatore take her home?" Bruno asked.

"He's right, Tony. You can't be distracted right now," Carlo replied.

The car pulled up to the warehouse.

*Thirty minutes later*

**Sabrina**

Salvatore arrived at my apartment a few minutes later. Feeling exhausted from dealing with Antonio, I waved Salvatore off from offering to walk me upstairs. I got out and waved goodbye. He pulled off just as I put the key in the lock. Suddenly, a hand grabbed me by the waist and covered my mouth as I tried to scream.

"Somebody help!" I shouted.

"Scream, and I'll hurt you."

I tried to fight, and he pulled me in a tight hold and placed a knife to my stomach. Feeling scared and nervous for my unborn child, I thought twice about my next movements.

"Are you sure you want to fight me on this, Bri Bri?"

To be continued…

* * *

s2read.com/u/4NXyPG with a host of characters intertwined.

What about dark romance that has everything from steamy romance, opposites attract, suspense, thriller, celebrity, and more **"Stolen:Fuertes Mafia Book 1"** https://books2read.com/u/mvZlgV

Catch up with favorite characters in this holiday short romance which includes spoilers. https://books2read.com/u/bzd59G

# INTRODUCTION OF 304 PUBLISHING COMPANY

We showcase authors writing African American, Interracial, Women's Fiction, Urban Romance, Erotic, and Contemporary Romance novels. Along with Thriller, Suspense, Poetry, Beauty, and Style Books. Thank you for taking the time out to visit. Join our mailing list to stay updated with new releases and blog posts.

# SPOTIFY PLAYLIST

## "ANTONIO AND SABRINA STRUCK IN LOVE SERIES"

1. Heather Headley- In My Mind
2. Love on the Brain –Rihanna
3. Cockiness –Rihanna
4. 7/11- Beyonce
5. Crazy In Love- Beyonce
6. Radioactive- Imagine Dragons
7. When We- Tank
8. 8. Insecure- Jasmine Sullivan
9. Ain't Too Proud to Beg- The Temptations
10. 10. You Keep Me Hanging On-The Supremes
11. 11. Be Without You- Mary J Blige
12. Fire and Desire- Rick James & Teena Marie
13. I'd Rather Go Blind- Etta James
14. Make You Feel My Love- Adele
15. Lost Without U- Robin Thicke
16. Apologize- One Republic

# AUTHOR BIO

Chiquita Dennie is an Author, Award winning Filmmaker and Podcast Host. Her first short film "Invisible" released in Summer 2017 and screened in multiple festivals and won for Best Short Film. Also, hosts a podcast that showcases the latest in Beauty, Business and Community called "Moscato and Tea." Her debut release of Antonio and Sabrina Struck In Love has opened a new avenue of writing that she loves.

Chiquita lives in Los Angeles, CA. Before she started writing contemporary romance, worked in the entertainment Industry on notable TV shows Dr Phil show, Tyra Banks show, American Idol, and Deal or No Deal. But her favorite job is the one she's now doing full time writing romance.

If you want to know when the next book will come out, please visit my website at http://www.304publishing.com, where you can sign up to receive an email for my next release.

# WHAT'S NEXT?!

Want to know what happens next?

Struck in Love 3 is available on Amazon now.

Reviews are the lifeblood of the publishing world. They're read, appreciated, and needed. Please consider taking the time to leave a few words on Amazon.

Sign up for updates and sneak peeks at the site below. www.chiquitadennie.com

# CATALOG RELEASES

The Early Years-A Prequel Short Story
Antonio and Sabrina: Struck in Love 1, 2, 3,4,5
Heart of Stone, Book 1 (Emery & Jackson)
Heart Of Stone Book 1.5 Emery &Jackson A Valentine's Day Short
Janice and Carlo: Captivated By His Love
Heart of Stone, Book 2 (Jordan and Damon)
Temptation
Heart of Stone, Book 3 (Angela and Brent)
Bottoms Up Heart of Stone, Book 3.5(Jessica and Joseph Short
Cocky Catcher
Bossy Billionaire
Love Shorts:A Collection of Short Stories
Joaquin Fuertes (The Fuertes Cartel Book 1)
Exposed (Salvation Society Novel)
Joaquin Fuertes (The Fuertes Cartel Book 2)
Refuel(A Driven World Novel)
Pressure(A Driven World Novel)

Until Serena(HEA World Novel)
Exposed (Salvation Society Novel)
Heart of Stone, Book 4 (Jessica and Joseph)
She's All I Need
Something Gaine( Romantic Comedy)